Homeless

Homeless

Jane Bow

QUATTRO BOOKS

The publication of *Homeless* has been generously supported by
the Canada Council for the Arts and the Ontario Arts Council.

 Canada Council   **Conseil des Arts**
for the Arts   du Canada

 ONTARIO ARTS COUNCIL
CONSEIL DES ARTS DE L'ONTARIO

Editor: Luciano Iacobelli
Cover Design: Natasha Shaikh
Typography: Sarah Varnam

Library and Archives Canada Cataloguing in Publication

Bow, Jane, author
    Homeless / Jane Bow.

 ISBN 978-1-988254-55-5 (softcover)

        I. Title.

PS8553.O8985H66 2018   C813'.54   C2018-903446-7
Published by Quattro Books Inc.
Toronto, Canada
www.quattrobooks.ca

Printed in Canada

For all those who have lost their way home

...A critical point poised between the chaotic and static states, the edge of chaos, (is) where the emergent response is most creative.

– Roger Lewin, *Complexity: Life At The Edge Of Chaos*,
University of Chicago Press, 2nd edition, 1999

One

I am a criminal. If discovered I could lose my children, my license to practice, maybe even my freedom. Kay and little Normie will need some way to understand, that's why I'm writing this, the whole truth and nothing but the truth, as it happened. When I'm finished I'll bury it in the back garden, under the petunias.

* * *

The woman slouching in the chair on the other side of my desk at St. Christina's Mental Health Centre smells of hospital soap and stale smoke. She is wearing a hospital gown and a men's blue bomber jacket with 'Dave' embroidered on one of its sleeves. Remnants of what must have been golden streaks paint the jagged ends of rich chestnut hair that has been hacked off at the shoulders. She uses it as a curtain, her eyes defiant blue, darting, behind it. I take no notice. All I want, on this snowy afternoon in early April, is to show her the quickest route out of here.

She refuses to tell anyone her name. Not police who caught her inside someone else's house, not court social workers or defence counsel, not even old Hammer Head, the supernumerary judge nicknamed for his blunt head and penchant for quick, shark-like judgements. When a week in jail did nothing to change her attitude the judge ordered a thirty-day psychiatric assessment, here. Usually I conduct these intake interviews inside my forensic psychiatric unit but I have had this woman brought to my office in the main hospital. I want her to see the metal detectors and locked doors that separate her from freedom.

Some of Canada's most dangerous offenders live here. Forty-eight year-old Lucy chopped up her baby daughter with a kitchen cleaver when she was eighteen. Her boyfriend came home to find her stuffing the tiny bloody limbs into freezer bags and fled, screaming, into the street. "He's so squeamish," she complained to the police, "I think I'm gonna have to leave him." Sweet, blond, thirty-year old Jimmy the Tooth bites people. Jeffrey Day shoved a woman into the path of an oncoming car. Maria may or may not have put paint thinner in her common-law husband's soup. God only knows what he had been doing to her. A neighbour discovered his body the following day. Maria was crouched in a stairwell repeating the only word she has uttered since: 'Bitch bitch bitch." And then there is big Stan, a psychopathic rapist who liked to slice up his victims before he murdered them. Today, if a mentally ill person is fit to stand trial and deemed to have known, during the commission of a crime, that what they were doing was wrong – and most do – they go to a normal prison. Thirty years ago however, criminals like Stan, Lucy and the others were found by the courts to be 'not guilty by reason of insanity' and hospitalized for life. The law that changed that was not retroactive. Hopefully a couple of days in the company of Lucy, big Stan and the others, will persuade Ms. Icognito to co-operate.

"I meet a lot of people with mental illness," I tell her, "but you're the only one who has ever claimed to see aliens." The question on our admission form is designed to catch malingerers.

"So?" She shakes back her hair. "Maybe lots of us see little green Martians all the time but prefer not to mention it. Or maybe it's a new phenomenon, a product of too many pesticides on suburban lawns."

"You live in the suburbs, Ms.?"

Her eyes become blue stones.

I fold my hands as if I do not have emails, requisitions, reports waiting, as if my telephone does not vibrate every three minutes, as if there is no gym to visit, no children to pick up before the daycare closes in less than two hours. A pile of psychology quarterlies I have not had time to read is in danger of slipping off the end of my desk. I ignore it.

"I can wait.' I give her a smile. "I'm the end of the line. I can wait for the rest of your life."

The stones glimmer, shift to the right, the left. Relationships between eye movements and the brain form a whole field of research, but what I see is calculation.

"Okay," she allows, "you can call me C."

"'C' as in Catherine or Carol or –?"

"'C' as in Seeing is Believing, Dr. Dolittle. And no, suburbia is not an address I'd choose." Her words are spat out in volleys. "My sister chose that route and look what happened to her. Condemned to life with Buzz Top. Lining up her SUV at the drive-through every morning, motor running. Waiting for her double double –" Her hair curtain closes. A giggle gurgles. "Oops, sorry, Doc. How do I know you drive an SUV?"

I make a note:

Articulate, intelligent.
Sassy = fear?

"So you have a sister."
Silence.
"You can tell me how old you are, at least."
She takes a partly smoked cigarette out of her jacket pocket and, holding it between her lips, bends her head, flicks on an imaginary lighter, and pulls in an imaginary lungful of smoke.

"How old do you think I am? Twenty-something: fresh out of school?" Manic laughter, strangled. "Thirties then: jilted, disillusioned, delusional?" An unplucked eyebrow lifts. "How 'bout a youthful forty?" Fake smile. "Sorry, Dr. Sweetmeat, a lady does not divulge her age."

"Oh? Well, I'm thirty-eight and I'm guessing we're about the same age."

She taps pretend ash off her cigarette onto

the floor, takes another drag and then loses interest, her eyes straying over my shoulder, past the spider plants crawling along my windowsill, out over St Christina's snow-smudged lawns to the streak of black water running down the centre of the St. Lawrence River's frozen flatness. Closer to shore light blue cracks zigzag across it. Any day now the ice will break up and the river will come alive. Longing flickers in C's eyes, then she blinks herself back to my washroom green office walls with their lacework of cracks, my degrees and the Monet water lilies Ernie bought to celebrate my appointment here last year, the youngest psychologist in charge of a forensic psychiatry unit in Canada. (Why haven't I taken the stupid picture down?)

"They took my clothes."

"To wash them."

She returns to the view. Somewhere in the bowels of St. Christina's the furnace comes on, rattling the white-painted metal radiator under the window. I wonder, can I use C's intelligence to cut a path through whatever brambles are choking out who she is?

"Look C, you need to understand that your sanity is not the issue here. My job is simply to assess whether you are fit to stand trial, and whether you were 'criminally responsible' at the time of your break-in. If the answers to these two questions are yes, the judge will send you back to jail for as long as it takes you to give him your name. Then you'll be charged with breaking and entering, tried and most likely convicted. If I find you unfit for court, or unable to appreciate the nature of your action and that it was wrong, you will remain here. Indefinitely."

Crow's feet around the woman's eyes deepen. She pulls on her cigarette.

"You're trying to scare me."

"No, just letting you know you can't win. Tell the judge your name and that you're sorry. He'll probably give you a suspended sentence –"

"Which means a criminal record and the ruination of my life, so no." Her stare could reseal the St. Lawrence ice. "I'm not sorry and I'm not a criminal."

"You were caught inside a century home full of antiques."

"So? Did I break anything to get in? No. Did I take anything? No. Were the house's new 'owners' even in the country at the time? No."

"What were you doing there?"

Her attention returns to her cigarette. "Meeting someone."

I nod towards her sleeve.

"Dave?"

"No, not Dave! He was against it. Waiting outside. He must have got away …" A smile leaks out of a corner of her lips, then drains away. "The person I went to meet is dead."

"I see." I close her file, look at my watch.

She assesses my face, hair, clothes.

"No, I don't think you do. See anything, Dr. –" My name, Dr. Elaine Price, is on the office door. She must not have noticed. Leaning down, she checks under the desk: "Purple pumps!" A caw of surprised laughter. "Dr. Pumps!"

Enough. I press my intercom button to summon an orderly and stand up. Blushing, that flood of blood to the cheeks, is a tendency no amount of education/therapy/relaxation can control. And sensible shoes are not a prerequisite for my job. Yes, I spent my formative fashion years in libraries, and yes, I like to shield myself in dark blue or grey suits with silk blouses, but shoes are my one indulgence: rich purple-blue Italian leather, deliciously pointed, high heels giving definition to my calves. I like the way these pumps tilt my hips forward, lend fluid grace to my walking.

There isn't enough time left to get to the gym. I'll stay here, use the late afternoon quiet to revisit the print-out of a computer memory stick police found zipped into an inner pocket of C's jacket, the only real information in her file. It's a story about a pioneer called Deirdre two hundred and sixty years ago, and reads like history brought to life. Written by C?

Deirdre's man, Neil MacIntyre, had run afoul of Scotland's British occupiers and been forced to join their army in North America to avoid jail. He hated the military, stamping in rigid redcoat lines through New England's virgin woods. *I don't know how I kept going through all that muddy, bloody, mosquito-ridden insanity,* he wrote to Deirdre. After Britain's General Wolfe finally defeated France's General Montcalm at Quebec in 1759, tracts of Nova Scotia's forested seashore were broken into land grants and offered to soldiers who had helped in the conquest. Neil chose a homestead a mile north of a new settlement at Chester.

It will be rough living for awhile, but Scotch Cove is beautiful, my sweet. There are salmon in the stream, and ducks, and deer in the woods, and fruit trees planted by a group of New Englanders who have already settled here. We will be free! And I will love you if only you will come to me now. Six gruesome weeks in a ship's hold crammed with sweating, retching, stinking humanity brought eighteen-year-old Deirdre to the quay at Halifax.

I sit back in my chair. Imagine the courage it must have taken to leave her family and everything she knew. Deirdre must be the dead person C was trying to meet inside the century home. I want to read on but the daycare is across town and I like to check in with the forensic unit's nurse on duty before leaving for the night. My staff, some of whom have been here as long as the oldest residents, run my forensic unit day-to-day but I need them to view me as part of their team. Also I'm curious to see how C is handling her fellow residents.

Smells of canned peas, potatoes and gravy reach me as soon as I let myself into the unit. Two rows of television screens behind institutional green curtains in our glassed-in monitoring station show the hall, bedrooms, lounge, and the dining room where my twenty-three charges are having dinner. Charlie, the duty nurse, and I watch Rosa and Mark glide back and forth behind them, delivering plates full of food, refilling water glasses. Keeping their eyes on hands, shoulders, faces.

"Hi New Girl!" Lucy's school girl squeak does not match her arthritic knuckles. Her bird-boned frame, lost inside a faded pink 'Roots' sweatshirt, and her wispy hair suggest frailty but her eyes, fixed on C who is sitting beside her, are predatorial . I feel myself tensing.

C ignores her.

"Oh, I get it," Lucy looks across at Maria and tips her head towards C. "She don't talk."

"Bitch," Maria looks away. Lucy lets out a spray of laughter, cuts it off.

"It's okay." She reaches for the arm of C's jacket. "'Bitch' is the only word Maria ever says."

C moves her arm away.

Rosa puts down a plateful of food. Lucy picks up her plastic fork.

Down at the other end of the table Harry and big Stan are discussing last night's hockey game, Stan jabbing the air with his fork, one jab per point, his big shaven head poking forward, eyes protruding. Every now and then Harry opens his mouth to say something, then thinks better of it. The rest of the men – even Radio, an elderly pedophile nicknamed because of the endless stream of commentary he can't help producing – concentrate on their mashed potatoes.

"Hi New Girl!" No body language, no tone or signal forewarn us as Lucy drives her fork straight down into the top of the hand C has left lying on the table.

"Hey!" The monitor shows C's stab of pain, her shock, her attacker's puckered glee, the rest of the diners frozen into a silent, open-mouthed tableau.

"Lucy!" Rosa's arm, bulky as a longshoreman's, jerks the mad woman's chair away from the table with her still in it. "Is that any way to treat your new neighbour?" Rosa's Jamaican accent, a song of patience, masks her intransigence.

Mark moves close to Stan. Charlie's and my breathing has quickened. My brain checks its horror, assesses the damage, plots its next move. Caged violence breeds faster than a virus but because our PMIs (persons with mental illness) have not been convicted of anything we are not allowed to treat them as prisoners, applying consequences to bad behaviour. Beyond administering daily drugs to control their impulses, all we can do is watch for warning signs, forestall incidents, try to talk people down before it's too late. Some are easy care, thank God, a few even functional enough to hold jobs in the community. Humans are not robots though, blood flows, hormones and tensions wax and wane, and drugs are not magic.

"New Girl's stabbed!" shouts Radio, "stabbed stabbed stabbed!"

"Shut up, you old turd." Stan does not take his eyes off the newcomer.

"Well, she won't even say hello." Lucy pouts.

Stan chuckles. "She's probably terrified, you vicious little psycho." His tongue runs along his lips.

"Talk about the pot calling the kettle black," says Charlie, beside me.

"You all right, honey?" Rosa asks C. "Let me see that hand."

Everyone watches C ignore the attendant, looking at Stan for at least half a minute, then slowly turning to Lucy. Dark circles make hollows of her eyes on the monitoring screen but only the small muscles at their outer edges sketch the shock and fear she will not acknowledge. Where, I wonder, has she learned this degree of emotional containment? Her skin is weather-thickened, her voice hoarse-edged, at odds with the sophisticated mind that must have written Deirdre's story.

"You touch me again," she tells Lucy, "any place, anytime, and I'll knock your little mouse voice right into the back of your head, I promise." She looks around the table. 'I'm hoping we understand each other?"

Lucy squeals, delighted. "Okay girlfriend!"

Stan's gaze is expressionless, blank-eyed. Never a good sign.

Ten minutes to get to the daycare: I order a twenty-four hour watch on Stan, in whom violence acts as an aphrodisiac, and sprint for the door. Poor Normie, I promised him a game of driveway hockey tonight. Running around in the cold air, slapping a puck and letting off steam are medicine for him, but now I will have to return to the hospital, file an incident report. I pause at the car to call Amanda, a grade twelve student who lives down the block – If I deliver seven-year old Kay and little Normie to the house, will she heat up a frozen casserole for them? – and thank God for this girl who, like me, appears to have no life of her own.

The skin on C's hand is not broken. As long as she refuses to give up her name, visions of lawsuits can stop dancing through my head. By the time I finish my paperwork all I can see in the window is my own reflection. It is after eight o'clock, too late to make it home in time for bedtime stories. Little Normie has not had a tantrum though or Amanda would have called. Kicking off my shoes, I try to shake out my shoulders, the back of my neck as tight as the day I defended my doctoral thesis, my nerves as strung as they were in high school, when popular girls played with bespectacled girls like me the way cats play with a trapped mouse.

C's file is still lying on my desk. Idly I flip it open. Is Deirdre's story fiction, C's way of channelling intolerable psychological pressures? Is she creating something she needs, a past in which to root herself? She loves Deirdre, that much is clear. I'll stop in to see her on my way home. Maybe, if her guard is down, I can pry loose some clues.

Forensic unit bedrooms are chipped and seedy: an iron bed, diarrhea green wooden chair and matching bedside table, a wooden armoire, a window reinforced with chicken-wire. Most patients stick cards or mementoes on their cupboard doors, or hang photographs or pictures on the walls. C's room is devoid of personality. Sitting cross-legged on her bed, she is reading a magazine, an ice bag covering the back of her hand, her bomber jacket enveloping her like a hug. Dare I admit to a tiny shot of vindictive hope? Maybe now C will agree to leave this leaky ship of wayward souls.

"How are you feeling?" I lean against the door frame.

C looks up, runs an appraising eye down to my shoes, says nothing.

"I've been enjoying your history of Deirdre MacIntyre. It's beautifully written."

"It's a diary! Private."

"Oh? Tell that to Anne Frank, Samuel Pepys, Dr. Johnson." Will comparing her to literary diarists help her to trust me? "I wish I could write like that."

"Pfff," She looks at the ceiling. "You hear that, Deir'?" She cocks an ear, listening, nodding.

No clear lines exist between mental disorder and what we call normal, and delusional disorder is not necessarily characterized by abnormal behaviour.

A sufferer's thought processes can be as intact as yours and mine, delusion taking over only in times of stress or threat. Does C know this?

"You did a lot of historical research on Deirdre."

"Nope."

"Well, somebody did."

She considers the bedroom walls. "Actually, if you think about it, there are three possibilities: one, I made up Deirdre's story; two, I wrote what I was told; or three –" She looks up, one eyebrow arched, "I'm clairvoyant."

"Possibilities two and three suggest that you have met this Deirdre. If this is true, why don't you tell me where?"

"Scotch Cove, Nova Scotia."

"Your family comes from the Maritimes?"

C gives me a 'nice-try' grimace.

"Why don't I save you some time, Doc? Deirdre MacIntyre does not come from my father's side. You won't be able to trace me through her name."

"How did you come to be in Nova Scotia?"

"Drove there."

"Recently?"

"That's for you to guess and me to know." Tinny laughter. "I had this dream car, a silver Mustang convertible."

"And you drove it to Scotch Cove?"

"Yup. Found the old house abandoned on

this hillside overlooking the sea, climbed some stairs to the loft, and heard Deirdre's voice: 'Ach, such a lovely man, my Neil.'" Her perfect Scottish brogue sends a shiver through me but her blue gaze, opaque as the March sky, offers no sign of shift. Neither has her body's stance changed, the way a person's often does when several personalities share a single body. So she's a mimic. Aren't all gifted writers?

"Ah, forget it, Deir'," she tells the ceiling. "It's written all over her expressionless face that this shrink doesn't believe you exist." She looks away, at the dark windowpane. "So why don't you fuck off, Super Doc –"

Rudeness can be part of a new resident's testing process. My best route forward is not to acknowledge or censure it, or strike back.

"Would you like a pen and some paper so you can go on with Deirdre's story?"

"No thanks."

Her disinterest is not feigned. Could this be because, having brought Deirdre to life, she now realizes that a mental construct, an imaginary friend, cannot fill the yawning hole in which she finds herself? If so, good.

"Your Deirdre is very real to you."

C looks at me, comes to a decision. Straightens her back as if she were not a ragged and homeless ward of the court consigned to my custody, as if we were two colleagues in a meeting.

"Look Doc, every person's reality is made

of what he or she feels and thinks, right? Take sex for example, having an orgasm. It happens because you are sexy. Why are you sexy? Because you feel sexy. You think sexy." Her words tumble one into the next, a waterfall of sound. "No sexy beautiful woman feeling, no orgasm. We feel/think therefore we come." Quick smile, a shaft of sunlight on the waterfall. "Same thing with knowing the dead. All you have to do is be open, let yourself feel –"

A cloud – something on my face? – shutters the light.

"Why am I bothering, Deir'? Tunnel vision never gets you outside the tunnel, Dr. Dumbnuts." Apparently though, she hasn't given up on me yet. "Okay, maybe orgasms aren't your thing, so let's say I'm here in my room and you're in the hall. I think of you but I can't see or hear or touch you. What makes you any more real to me then than Deirdre? You're both my brain's interpretation of a swirling mass of subatomic energies – a repressed, seething mass in your case, if you'll pardon my saying so."

"Are you telling me that to you, both Deirdre and I are equally present?"

"No." Curt smile. "My vote goes to Deirdre. This is the nightmare."

"So let me help you wake out of this nightmare." I pause, letting the word bounce around us. "Start with your dream car. What happened to it?"

"Who knows, Twinkle Toes? I sold it for $2,000."

"$2,000, for a Mustang!"

The 'Dave' jacket's shoulders rise.

"My credit card was maxed out so I sold it to a gas jockey in Quebec. He thought he'd died and gone to Heaven."

"And then?"

Another shrug. "It was December. A bus to Toronto had stopped at the gas station."

"And still you didn't call home?"

She looks out again at the darkness.

"Home, now there's a concept: a place to hang your needs, cuddle your lover, shine up his ego, sweep your doubts into the cracks. Any cracks in your home, Dr. Perfect?" Imprisoned by whatever psychological mayhem rules them, PMIs are usually unaware of their effect on those examining them. C's smirk tells me this is not the case with her. But behind her bravado fear is also prowling.

"Don't you care what happens to you, C?"

She looks at her hand. "Since when does caring take you anywhere?"

An opening?

"Caring is learned," I tell her. "When a little girl hurts herself, someone who cares kisses her better, and in so doing sets a model – we call it a schema – in the little girl's brain of what caring is, and how it produces feel-good chemistry –"

"Right, so riddle me this, Dr. Strangelove: when exactly does your caring schema make any difference whatsoever to anything in the real world?

You'll tell me you care, that you want to do the best job you can with me, so will your warders. But let's be honest. You, the police, the judge, none of you cares who I am. Your job stops at finding out my name and why this chick didn't give a shit that day at the house, and is it pathological –?"

"Whoa." I push away from the doorframe and put up a hand.

"No, step out of those purple pumps, Doc. Put on my beat-up runners and think: You just got caught inside a million-dollar stone house. Are you going to tell anyone your name? They can't charge you with anything if they don't know your name, and are they really going to keep me here or in jail, eating out of the public trough, forever? As for whatever else you hope to find out, news flash honey: who I am, how and what I think, how I operate my life, that's private, personal and confidential." Despondent, confrontational, sharp, quick as a razor blade.

I am not out of my depth.

"Good night C." Enigmatic smile. Please God, help me find some way to back it up.

Two

'Home,' now there's a concept. Six months after Ernie's departure, mine still feels like a body from which a limb has been amputated. The children are asleep. I spoon leftover chicken casserole into a bowl and eat it mindlessly at the kitchen counter. If Ernie were here we might have a Scotch and I would tell him about the day's catastrophes and about C.

No I wouldn't. Ernie is an accountant, not interested in my 'mental junkyard' and anyway I'm bound by an oath of confidentiality.

Too wound up to go to bed, I switch on the backyard floodlight. Spring's first warmth has shrunk the snow cover but tonight it's cold again. I put on my ski jacket and gloves, find my rubber gardening boots and the shears in the garage. My gardens along the privacy fences are a shadowland, under a rising half moon, of floral ghosts I did not have time to cut back last fall.

Ernie and I chose this house because outside the backyard gate an access path leads to parkland along the river. We imagined taking the children on nature walks, gathering wildflowers, carrying a canoe down to the water. None of this has happened. Once when I did open the back gate Kay, who was four, cowered behind my legs. The tall grasses, prickly thistles, the jumble of overgrown bushes looked 'scary', she cried.

Virginia creeper that just a few months ago glowed brilliant crimson up the back fence is a tangle of naked vine now. A half dozen dead corn stalks rustle in the centre of the vegetable patch. Ernie and I grew vegetables so Kay and Normie would understand that our food comes from the earth, and life and death are a cycle. Last summer pea plants latched onto and climbed up the growing corn, squashes nestled into their shade, the corn-pea-squash triumvirate designed to teach our children about the interdependency of all living things. Watering, weeding and caring for plants would bring fresh tomatoes, carrots … and long lines of ants goose stepping towards the back door. Normie hates vegetables. Kay is allergic to peas. Now, snipping in the crisp night air, I tug out the vines, haul brittle remains off to the composter, bring order to chaos.

Order: the trellis up which health, stability, happiness can be made to grow. My mother believed that, which is why I never told her anything important. Once, in grade eleven, students were to vote for a team to represent the school in a local cable television general knowledge contest. Routinely the top of my class, I was so excited. But when team members' names were posted, mine was not among them. "If only you wore contacts, Elaine," commented Miranda, our class's elected representative. If she had known, my mother would have stormed into the principal's office and made a scene, to 'put things right'. Mothers, what central power they hold in our lives.

It is what happens to us however, and the neural pathways that are set up as a result, that define who we are. Horror, hurt, betrayal, disappointment, embarrassment, denial, visceral pain may eventually be forgiven. They are never forgotten. I sought refuge in science and the cello, where everything is ordered, nothing left to happenstance. By the time I reached university the nature of recurring patterns fascinated me. Why do groups of girls victimize innocent classmates? And why, in spite of their meanness, do their victims pine for their acceptance? It was a short hop from there into a doctorate in forensic psychology and the study of relationships between morality and the order of law.

I hack at the creeper, taking grim pleasure in ripping out the wild and useless. Wish I could do the same at work. Find a human composter for Lucy and Stan. A dead branch pulls a chunk of my hair out of its pony tail. I stop to disentangle it, looking up. Stars blink in the darkness surrounding the moon. Their light travels for years to reach my eyes. C is right, all life is really nothing more than a kaleidoscope of energies. Patterns our senses perceive of colour, sound, smell, taste, feelings are energy shaped by who we are and what we know. Really there is only infinity, Western astrophysicists and ancient Eastern philosophers agree on that. Well. I may be a scientist but I can only believe what I see, what I touch. A star as a twinkle of light is as far as I can go.

My professional success has little to do with my training. When you grow up in a house fuelled by the pursuit of order and a schoolyard run on power, if you are smart enough to keep your thoughts packed away inside the safety of your mind, your perceptions sharpen, your inner voice whispers intuition. You learn to listen, to trust it, the way you do your car engine. Psychology provides the steering wheel, brakes, head and tail lights.

Cut back to its roots, the Virginia creeper leaves the back fence looking naked. Hard to imagine that two months from now new shoots will find purchase and climb. I turn to my rose bushes, snip off a shrivelled bud and raise it to my nose to see if any fragrance might have survived the winter. Ernie gave me roses once, before we had kids. Now there is only my breath vaporizing and the scents of cut vine, cold earth and rotting snow.

Sipping hot chocolate and watching the news, cold glowing in my cheeks, I look across at Ernie's empty chair. Once, not that long ago, he would have met my gaze, his ginger hair sitting up naturally in the spikes other men have to sculpt with gel. A line from C's story comes to me: ... *He stroked my stomach, my thighs, places no other person had ever touched before. I heard myself gasp at the pleasure of it and began, slowly, to move with the rhythm of a current that was building, eddying ...*

Ernie would lie in wait for me outside the

university library. Why, I could not comprehend. Boys had not featured in my high school life, dating/love/sex a mystery I couldn't begin to crack. Ernie was a stocky fireplug of a guy who had managed to get himself onto the football team. We started going out to movies followed by hamburgers and long discussions. I started taking an interest in what I was wearing, visiting make-up experts at The Bay, and it was fun. Ernie had his own place and sometimes we would cook there, laughing because neither of us had a clue, and talking about what was going on in the world and what it meant, and our futures. He touched me, casually at first, with a sureness that dissolved my confusion. Then on New Year's, at a football team party, we drank too much, took a cab to his apartment, and he found his way into me, grunting, skin slapping, my legs flailing above us. Not much in it for me but I loved it anyway. I was a woman now. Over time we learned each other's bodies and how to make them work, and thought we were pretty tuned in to each other, both in and out of bed. When I got pregnant with Kay, we married.

Three years later Normie was born. Ernie pictured them throwing a football, going to games. He would teach his son everything he needed to know on and off the field. Normie co-operated by catching a ball much earlier than is normal, delighting his father. What he couldn't do was handle tension. If anything much is demanded of Normie, he screams. An exaggerated case of the terrible two's, said the doctor. Not autism or Asperger's Syndrome because Normie expresses and responds to emotions. When he was smaller Ernie would hold him tight in his arms until the tantrum's energy drained away, like air out of a paper bag, but our son is growing, rages striking every time he tries something new and fails, and he is too big to hold now. Time-outs in his room do not calm him until he has exhausted himself by destroying everything in sight.

How many times have I tried to explain to his father that this imbalance in our little boy may simply be the result of some brain connections developing late? Functional MRI scans all come back normal. He might grow out of this. Or, he may have food sensitivities. Keep him off sugar, advised the doctor. Easier said than done if you take your children to a movie or a fast food joint or a birthday party. Then there's Hallowe'en, Christmas, Easter. Anyway, is sugar the problem, or is the stew of chemicals in all our foods and air and water messing up our son's intricate little body in ways no one knows how to diagnose? Or are electronics – cell phones, tablets, computer routers – irradiating his delicate little brain cells?

Whatever the cause, last fall the chasm between Ernie's dreams and reality finally swallowed him. That's how I see it. He claims that I am either a hopeless mushball of a mother at home or an absent, negligent parent who spends too much time at work. Our fights made the worst possible environment for

Normie so when a new accounting job came up three
hours away in the city, Ernie quit the battlefield. He
takes the children for a weekend once a month and
it's better this way. Poor Kay needs more attention,
less strife. Little Normie is in junior kindergarten and
I am hoping a structured routine and peaceful home
life will keep him stable. If only I can impose some
order on my life. Not like tonight.

The television newscaster is talking about
teetering economies and plunging stock markets.
If Ernie were sitting across from me he would be
singing his endless round of economic blues. I should
get rid of his chair. Put a potted plant in its place, a
colourful, flowering one, hibiscus maybe.

In the meantime I am still wide awake. Why
don't I end this day by getting a start on tomorrow?
My laptop is right here in my briefcase. I'll make a
few plans while C's story is fresh in my mind. Her
name is what I need. So:

1. Ask police to do a land title search on the stone
   house inside which she was caught. See if there
   is any connection between it and a Deirdre
   MacIntyre from Nova Scotia. C's written rendition
   of, and reliance on this character may be the key to
   sorting threads in her tangled psyche.
2. Ask C where Deirdre was during her break-in.
3. Give C a tape recorder and some tapes. Her
   conversations with Deirdre suggest that in spite
   of her reticence communication is central to her.

Lucy and Maria are the only other women in my unit and neither of them is sane enough to offer companionship. Maybe C will spend her long useless hours talking to the tape recorder. Every bedroom is monitored by a security camera and often the body will betray clues that the mind needs to hide.

4. Her hair streaks look about six months old. Ask police to search for a female, chestnut-haired owner of a silver Mustang who disappeared sometime during the last couple of years. How many of those can there be on file? And computers can match missing persons reports to social insurance numbers to credit card statements and bank accounts.

Once I have her name C's irascible wall of self-protection will not take long to crumble, exposing whatever has landed her here. Fear will have something to do with it, it always does. If we could harness human fear, we could fuel the whole planet with it. But fear of what, I wonder, and did it take her sanity?

Three

I dunno about this recorder, Deir'. What kind of person wants you to give up your thoughts to a machine? C's disembodied voice sounds younger than she looks, vulnerable.

Pause.

Yeah, you're right, it will help while away the hours, and what's wrong with them knowing the reason I climbed up the front wall of a house that a piece of paper says belongs to a couple of federal civil servants who don't even live in it? Who only come down to play pioneer on summer weekends.

How many times did I risk hitchhiking along the highway to get there? Remember the night a car full of drunken students stopped and I had to run into the fields, corn husks rustling like bones all around me?

A chuckle.

Who planted the great sprawling maples along the front drive, Deir'? I'd try to time my visit so I'd have all day to walk the property, a carpet of red, gold, orange leaves underfoot. No one could see me. I'd smell the last of the wild roses nodding by the front door and look in through the windows. The house is more than a hundred and fifty years old, built of rubble stone Neil's and your descendants must have carried themselves.

Behind it, at the bottom of the lawn, there is

Jane Bow

a sugar bush and one day a few weeks ago I waded
through the heavy spring snow, using tracks left by
deer because God knows no human had been back
there in a very long time. There hadn't even been car
tracks in the driveway all winter. Huge maple trees
– some of them must have been a couple of hundred
years old – were scarred where taps had been
hammered in long ago to catch the spring sap, but
I guess civil servants don't go in for sugaring. The
old log sugar shack was falling down, its cast iron
cauldron tipped up on its side, wearing a cap of snow.
Inside it a curtain of cobwebs hid some little animal's
poo. The pot's outside was still charred from the fires
kept burning day and night to boil the sap, and for
the first time in years I got so excited! It was as if
you were right there with me, Deir'. I could smell the
burning hardwood, hear the sap popping as it boiled
down into syrup. So the next week I brought some
pot cleaner, half a dozen metal spouts, a hammer and
some coffee cans to hang on the trees. And talked
David into coming with me.

   Once last year he came later in the spring,
when the trilliums – trillia? – were out in the woods,
little white, lilac-veined miracles, and there was great
big David bending over them, looking and looking,
not touching because an Ontario forest guide he'd
read in the library said it was against the law. I called
to him. He looked up, delicate flowers nodding all
around him, and on his face was a beautiful smile. I
would have made love to him that day, there among

the trilliums, it seemed exactly the right thing to do, but when I went to him, put my hand on his arm, moving close into his musty man scent, he tensed. He was aroused, I heard it in his breathing, but tenderness must have spelled danger to David then. His eyes, meeting mine, looked like a hunted deer's, and he shambled away.

Throat clearing.

This spring we collected the sap and piles of wood and built a fire. Neither of us had ever made maple syrup before but David had read up on it at the library so we'd brought sleeping bags because you have to keep the fire going day and night. And next morning, sure enough, we had syrup, a few bits of grit and some ash in it, but oh! (Laughter) We spread some on the snow, just like you used to do, Deir', and it turned into maple taffy. Have I ever tasted anything so delicious?

Long pause.

Okay Dr. Pump-a-Dump, I might as well tell you about David since ... (brief chortle) you'll never find him. And even if you did ... (another chuckle.) He's tall, big chest, long arms, and a hug from him is a place to get lost in because the fact is some of us are builders in this life, and some are seers, thinkers, knowers of stuff. David is all of the above – brain like a physicist-chemist-engineer – he built me a platform tent in the ravine, a cot, a little propane stove, a lamp, a bike with saddle bags, all of it made from parts he'd scavenged from the local dump or on his night trips into the rich parts of the city. You could say he built me a life.

More throat clearing.

You'll want to know where we met. At the railing on the Bloor Street Viaduct, one midnight. I was on the outside of the steel cables they've put up to keep people from jumping. Car lights streaming up and down the Don Valley Parkway below me were rivers of light, white coming, red going and there was me, wearing a new blue Holt Renfrew dress, hanging on and scared to death the brand new high heels I was wearing would slip – though why would that matter if I was planning to let go? – All I could think was that the fall would take forever, time slowing to a crawl the way it does on a roller coaster when they've locked you into your seat and the car is clicking up the first incline and there is no more choice, no way to stop it. I'd fall and fall and fall, waiting, waiting to hit the pavement, to bounce off a windshield or a front bumper or onto the road between cars. To be run over, but maybe not killed. And the poor driver, some middle aged lady on her way home from a game of bridge, would never ever get over it. It was April, not cold, but my fingers on the steel wire had gone numb.

David came pedalling over the bridge on one of his homemade bicycles, its saddle bags stuffed because that's how he lives: goes out on his bike late at night to collect food and explore rich people's garbage, sleeps late then makes coffee and cooks whatever he found the night before. "It's amazing what the grocery stores and restaurants and bakeries throw out," he marvels, "there's enough food on any night in Toronto to feed a starving nation." He spends his afternoons in a public library reading poetry, physics, philosophy, archeology, Agatha Christie – whatever he feels like. Anyway, when he caught sight of me teetering outside the bridge railings, he stopped.

"Hi," he said, as if a woman in a ball gown teetering there in the middle of the night was nothing unusual. He got off his bike to lean over the railing beside me. I tensed but he just shook his head at the stream of car lights below. "Where can they all be going at this time of night?"

"To work work work, to make a buck buck buck." It just popped out in time to the beat of the traffic below.

He laughed, a funny deep sound that seemed to surprise him as much as me, then just stood there watching the flows of light.

"You want to get a cup of coffee?" he asked after awhile. "There's an all-night doughnut store I usually go to."

I looked down. Let go and I'd be gone. Down, down, the thought dizzying, terrifying. What if I let go by accident? What if I didn't really want to do this but my hands didn't know that? I'll tell you, Doc, balancing on that railing between death and yesterday's life, you are paralyzed. Removed, no longer welcome, in your own mind, either here or there.

David must have sensed something because now he was reaching up, his hands around mine on the steel wire, bringing warmth. And now he was taking my forearm, anchoring it with one hand, loosening my frozen fingers with the other, moving me down the line of cables, one hand then the other, my feet following obediently until I was standing on terra firma, not sure whether the arms around me, the warm puffs of breath on the top of my head and the smells of wood fire and apples belonged to a strange man on Bloor Street or whether I had let go and this was my guardian angel taking me to Heaven.

He helped me onto the seat of his bicycle and I held onto him, my cheek against his back, its muscles rippling as he pedalled over the bridge. At the coffee shop, his mouth full of jelly doughnut, he told me he liked my dress and he had this big open face with black stubble and beautiful black wavy hair and I heard myself laugh and then suddenly there I was in Dunkin' Donuts laughing and laughing then bawling, tears dropping onto the blue dress.

Long pause.

You'll say I mustn't really have wanted to jump, I can hear you, Dr. Dream Team. Isn't that why you've given me this tape recorder, so that salient facts about who I am and the nature of any depravities lurking behind my tangled hair and criminal tendencies will leak out through my distraction? Speaking of hair, Doc, I blame mine for my being stuck in here. I mean look at it: curly, thick as a horse's mane; let it fly around, get a little matted and presto, I must be crazy, right?

David trimmed my hair with barber's scissors he found at the dump's reuse centre. Then we would sneak into a hospital near our ravine and steal a shower. David would tell me I looked like a model and use his welfare cheque to buy us bacon and eggs in the cafeteria.

A chuckle.

One day in the cashier's line he turned to me.

"Nice to see Uncle Charles feeling a little better."

"Huh?" I wondered if his mind had slipped a gear. He was wearing jeans and a red and brown plaid shirt and a V-necked black sweater under his blue bomber jacket, also a slightly stained blue bow tie with black polka dots. This and his thick black, slightly receding, still wet hair combed sideways, made him look like a chunky Mr. Dressup.

"Uncle Chas." He rolled his eyes hard right. The cashier, wearing a plastic tag that said 'Supervisor', was taking too much interest in us. "Isn't it great to see him sitting up at last?"

"Oh! Yes! Especially since only last night they told us he might not make it." I raised my eyes to Heaven. "Thank You, dear Lord."

David looked down, staring hard at his bran muffin, his lips quivering towards a smile. The

Supervisor must have thought he was trying not to cry.

"Well isn't that wonderful."

Uncle Charles' progress became part of our weekly trip down the cafeteria food line.

Me: "Do you think Uncle Chas'll make it through his surgery?" Impending tears, daring David.

David: No words, his large hand reaching over to cover mine on the tray.

Supervisor, eyes compassionate: "Good luck, dears."

Next week, Supervisor: "How's your uncle?"

Me: "Better. A little."

David, one eye always on the practicalities: "It's going to be a long haul though."

Me: "Yes, his heart's stable but now they think his bladder may be ruptured."

David had appeared at my tent the night before with a twenty four-inch flat screen television – an old lady in Forest Hill had thrown it out – and a little gas-powered generator – he has about six, left over from the millennium Y2K scare – and we had watched an ER team fix someone's bladder in the nick of time.

Chuckling fades. Long pause.

Anyway, a few weeks after we made the maple syrup, I thought why not go back to the house? Be with you again, Deir'. Maybe find a way in, to see your spinning wheel.

The sun was just reaching the top of the trees

when we arrived, throwing eerie shadow patterns across the snow on the front lawn, turning it into such a loveless, forlorn black and white place. Branches of an old ironwood, the maples and a blue spruce were whispering to each other. I reached for David's hand and when he gave it to me I sensed trust, and pleasure. And then we were passing the house, following the path down into the maple woods, to the sugar shack. Making love on the sleeping bags we had left there, amid lingering smells of burning wood and maple taffy, a stumbling fumbling first time in a long, long time for David, which made it so rich, so sweet and precious –

Sharp intake of breath.

Why am I spilling all this? What business is it of yours, Dr. Open-the-Doors?

Sigh.

Well, what the hell. In for a penny, right Deir'?

Someone had left an upstairs casement window ajar. A line of metal hooks sunk into the mortar between the stones at the front of the house reached nearly as high as the sill. They would have been used to attach a wooden front porch, David told me. I had said nothing about the plan I was formulating but he always just knows things, the way you sometimes know someone's going to knock on your door just before they do, or the way a plant knows when you love it.

Shaky new breath.

So I'm standing there, shivering in the cold, looking up, so scared of heights. But then I thought of you, Deir', and of your daughter's sons and daughters who had cut and stripped this house's wooden beams, and how could I not climb?

The granite grazed my cheek with cold and my fingers grasping the iron hooks stiffened with cold. The soles of my running shoes felt as if they would slip.

"Look up," said David. So I reached up to one hook, then the next, and I could hear his breathing as he watched from below, ready to catch me. Until I could pull the window wide open and heave myself in over the sill.

Half-light turned the bedroom's four-poster bed and old-fashioned highboy dresser into a study of greys. Silver-framed ancestors glared out of starched collars and cinched waists. Whose relatives? Mine? The civil servants 'owners' had bought the house furnished. Or was this an auction purchase to 'antique' the room? Grimness as decor.

Something moved. The skin on my neck tightened. I turned my head. A blotch of white in the dressing table's oval mirror, framed by a mess of hair turned too. We let out our breath.

From the top of the stairs the living room, in early morning shadows, looked just as it must have a century and a half ago, as if the builders of the house were still upstairs in bed or, more likely, out fetching wood for the cooking hearth, or tending to their livestock or the fire in the sugar shack. Had the giant wooden rocker by the hearth, and the decoration plates mounted on the rail above the dining table, come from Scotland, via Nova Scotia?

When finally I screwed up enough courage to go down, there on the other side of the hearth, just where you told me it would be, was your spinning wheel, Deir', with its big wheel and low frame. My fingers found the brass plaque on the cross beam. It was too dark to read the engraving, but you'd already told me what it said:

> 'Presented to
> Mrs. Deirdre MacIntyre
> With Everlasting Gratitude,
> By Captain Jonathan Prescott
> On Behalf of
> His Royal Highness George III
> At the Town of Chester
> On This Day of Our Lord July 30, 1783
> God Save The King.'

And oh Deir', when I laid my hand on the wheel your hands had worked, when I closed my eyes and breathed in smells of dampness and woods and more than two hundred and thirty years of cooking fires –

But then someone was pounding on the door, voices, male, female, not David's, shouting. A key scraped in the front door lock, boots thundered on the pine floor. I could have tried to run out the back into the woods but I just stood there. A flashlight beam blinded me. Please God, I thought, let David get away.

You can imagine the rest: my arms being yanked behind me, steel handcuffs clinking, light searching the room, the grounds outside. But I had disturbed nothing and there was only me.

Pause.

So what exactly am I criminally responsible for, Doc?

And where do we go from here? Jail? Before coming here I shared a cell with a fourteen-year old found guilty of smoking a joint on a street corner at midnight after the court had put her on probation for fighting. Silly twit. Better lock her up though, get tough on crime, expose her fledgling little teenage soul to hardened addicts. Or what about the pregnant woman who was sentenced to house arrest in her upstairs apartment for passing bad cheques? She couldn't work so she got behind in her rent, couldn't afford food. She asked for help but nothing happened until, stuck in her apartment during a heat wave, she died. Like I told you, Doc, caring has nothing to do with how the world works.

What's that, Deir'?

Pause.

Yes, I know some people care. A Sally Ann lady showed up today with a pair of jeans for me, and this white blouse with frills down the front – who does she think I am, Faith Hill? – And David cares, I know that.

Another pause. What sounds like a sniff.

Shh. Cry and one of the Soft Shoes will see me on the monitor and come running: "What's wrong honey does your poor hand hurt why won't you tell us your name you can trust us you're going to have to trust somebody." On and on, one after another, all of them wearing Skate-A-Thon, Walk-A-Thon, Cancer Can Be Beaten do-gooder t-shirts and those sneak-up-on-you crepe soled shoes. "Hush now, honey. You want something to calm you down?"

So shut the fuck up, C.

Cup of coffee, piece of toast,
white hours stretching, who's the ghost, Doc
me or you?

* * *

My late afternoon reflection, in the window of my office, looks tired, or are those shadows under her eyes black clouds massing above the river? Three days have passed since my first interview with C. I have been telling myself that leaving her alone, having my staff watch and listen as she gets to know her community here, is the most efficient strategy, that my daily steamroller of emails, voicemails, reports and meetings, my levering, cajoling, badgering and pleading for my unit's share of the hospital's shrinking budget have no bearing on the delay. But bureaucracy rules, that's the truth: its ever escalating demands suck at my stamina.

Rattling trolleys, prattling visitors, hurrying nurses and doctors and orderlies have deserted the hospital's wide hallways by the time I am ready to pick up my children from daycare. Only St. Christina the Astonishing remains. Patron saint of the mentally disturbed, she smiles beatifically, her white plaster eyes following me as my heels tap across the hospital's front foyer outside my forensic unit. Our hospital's founders, the Sisters of St. Christina, installed statues of her on every floor as beacons of hope. A twenty-one-year old victim of a massive seizure in the 1150, St. Christina rose again at her funeral (somehow managing to hammer on her casket) and said she had visited Purgatory. God had given her a choice. She could stay with him or return to life to purge the sins of people who were suffering terribly in God's halfway house. For the next fifty-three years she entered blazing furnaces, freezing water, always emerging unscathed, until she died of natural causes. Eight hundred years later the government's need for psychiatric hospital beds and the nuns' need for funds have swept Catholic miracles out of this institution, but I like to think the Sisters' faith and the sweet breath of their dedication are not so easily expunged.

Except on my ward apparently. Trouble is an acrid-smelling, diaper-dragging moron of a presence as soon as I click through the unit's double-locked doors. My patients should be having dinner, or safely installed in front of The Price Is Right, or playing cards under the supervision of – I glance at the roster on the wall – Mike and May. Canned laughter comes down the hall from the lounge but Lucy's bedroom door is closed. C is hovering in her doorway. Lucy's door opens and May comes out.

"Oh, Doctor." Seeing C, she lowers her voice. "We thought you had gone home." A large muscled, greying ex-reform school matron, May somehow manages to look down her nose even though I am as tall as she is with my shoes on, making me feel that the blame for whatever has gone wrong lies squarely on my ignominious, post-adolescent shoulders.

I look past her into the bedroom. Lucy looks back at me, her little body barely raising the blankets on her bed, her eyes bright as nails.

No one warned me, when I took this job, about sexual 'liaisons' between Stan and Lucy. They appear to happen in the shower room. Is it consensual coupling? Can a man like Stan have healthy sex? There are never any overt signs of violence. Neither of them ever speaks about it, boasting or complaining, but the whole affair is a minefield that could blow anytime. What on earth to do? I have tried all the medications I can legally prescribe.

Steam billows out of the shower room. Maria peeks out of it into the hall, whimpering.

"Bitch bitch bitch."

Oh dear God, was she in there too while they were at it? May goes to her.

"You're all right, sunshine. Go on into your bedroom. No one will bother you there." She turns to C. "Do you need anything? Would you like to join the others in the lounge, or do you want to get ready for bed too?"

C shoots a look at me and withdraws.

"How was this allowed to happen?" I clip my voice, commanding respect.

"Mike noticed that Stan was not in the lounge –"

"Noticed? How can you mislay Stan? And what about Steve in the monitoring station? Didn't he see where Stan went?"

"Well you know there is that blind spot just inside the lounge –"

"Oh for pity's sake." But my staff has to watch and listen and tend to medications while also forestalling errant behaviours, soothing unbalanced psyches, and cleaning up inevitable accidents that are side-effects of heavy drug doses. All on a pay scale that makes waitresses look rich. Further, I'd like to meet the medical researcher who concluded that anti-depressants dull the sex drive. Let him or her take a night shift here, sort through who really did what to whom. "I guess there's no way of knowing whether you got to them in time?"

May looks most impatient when she feels threatened.

"All I can tell you for certain, Doctor, is that Lucy is not complaining."

"And Stan?"

"Mike took him back to watch TV with the others."

Secure in the knowledge of his kingship, testosterone build-up released, until next time. As for Lucy, there is never any physical damage so Stan can't be assaulting her. And she looks so smug afterwards. Does she glory in her sexual power, whispering seductively to him in the hallway after dinner? Or is the source of her smugness a perverted joy in having broken the rules, or worse, in having been victimized? There is no way to know. Lucy is post-menopausal, thank God. I look at my watch.

"File an incident report if you think it's warranted, May. I'll sign it in the morning."

A cold east wind is tearing apart the clouds above the river, whining through the telephone wires in the parking lot, shaking the lamp standard – truly a night in which Purgatorial demons dance.

Four

C looks washed and pressed. Her hair, tied back in a ponytail, adds age to the set of her cheek and jaw bones, and so far this morning there has been no sassiness, fakery or arrogance. Good. We are in the forensic unit's rose-coloured consultation room. No water lilies, no view of the river, no window at all, just a chipped metal desk, a computer, a filing cabinet. I have cleared someone's leftover cardboard coffee off the table at which we are sitting. Today I need to make some headway, find a way to get this woman out of here.

"About your friend David," I glance down at the transcript Jacklyn, my office assistant, has typed of C's tape. "You say he was a big man, big chest, long arms, and 'a hug from him was a place to get lost in.' You make love with him in the woods. In your diary young Deirdre and big beautiful Neil make love in a mountain glade." I smile. "Write what you know, isn't that what they say?"

C says nothing, her blue eyes expressionless. I scroll down through my notes. Two can play the silence game. Seconds tick into minutes.

"You want me to hate this place." A telltale jiggle has started in C's knee. "'Great,' you probably thought when that psychotic little Anthony Perkins-wannabe stabbed me with her fork." She wiggles the fingers on her damaged right hand and winces.

The bruise on the back of it has swollen into a purple hillock, its edges yellowing. "And I don't mind telling you – because the bedroom camera will have picked it up – that after you left that first night I lay there so scared my arms and legs were twitching, my heart pounding because did you see the look in that little fiend's eyes?"

Pure, radiant malevolence, I know it well.

"Do I have you to thank you for the needle the Soft Shoe finally delivered? All the next day my brain was so sluggish, so easily led. If I stay here that will be my future, won't it Doc, attacks followed by sedatives. Because there's something Very Bad about that guy Stan too. Your cameras don't catch much, you know. He's always brushing against me in the blind spot in the lounge doorway, then this morning as we were coming out of the dining room he patted my ass. Did anyone see that? Apparently not."

"You're frightened."

"Well, say Stan does do something to me, what happens to him? Nothing, right? Like when Lucy stabbed me."

"We are very vigilant, especially where Stan and Lucy are concerned." I hear the words' hollowness, because there is no way to stop Stan from whispering descriptions of what he will do to anyone who takes his chair in the lounge, or the magazine he wants to read. I try to look reassuring. "If properly medicated –"

"But how do you know Stan takes his pills?

What if he's holding them in his mouth then spitting them into the toilet? And Lucy showed me the blind spots in our bedrooms, right underneath the door –"

"So let me help you, C."

She chews her bottom lip. I sit back in my chair.

"Let's talk about your family – no names. What can you tell me about your life growing up?" Behaviour is deeply determined by genetics, environment and early conditioning, so who knows, she may let slip a clue to her identity.

She looks at the walls, bored.

"Comfortable suburban house, a TV in every room, father and mother at work. 'Bye honey,' called up the stairs at 7:30 am, 'Love ya!' In my suburb the human psyche was a parking lot, yellow lines ordering where thoughts were to be left while consumers flocked to the mall."

"And you would have preferred?" I keep my voice light.

"How should I know? Baking cookies, washing the floor together?"

Could I be right: Deirdre's story was C's attempt to create what she did not have – family closeness? I move us towards the present.

"You sound lonely. Does that have anything to do with your visit to the Bloor Street bridge, I wonder, all alone in an expensive new dress?"

No reply.

"Teetering, scared to death your shoes would

slip, and then along comes David."

Silence.

"Okay, then at least tell me, where was Deirdre while you were on the bridge? You had just driven east, discovered her and spent time getting to know her, so where was she that night, C?"

Her face closes, obstinate, confused and bereft. Good. Through pain to truth – though not today, it seems.

* * *

Down at the bottom of the lawns the last of the day's light glances off the white St. Lawrence. Outside my office window a pair of wrens have joined the chickadees at the feeder tray I have stuck onto the glass. I smear it with peanut butter to attract these downy little birds and their round, clear, excited spring song. They flutter off into the dusk when I open my laptop.

I can stay here as long as I want tonight, catching up and making notes, clarifying my thinking before heading to the gym. It's Friday and Ernie is picking up the children from daycare for a weekend in the city. They'll be on the road by now, stopping at McDonald's on the highway in spite of our sugar restrictions, both kids high on excitement. My flock here will be sitting down for dinner, Stan and Lucy paying no attention to each other, according to my staff. C is keeping to herself.

She loves homeless, unfindable David. Why? What had sent her careening out of her daily routine all the way to Nova Scotia where, communing with her past, she tried and failed to fill a hole so deep it took her finally to the Bloor Street Viaduct? Where David found her.

I click into my emails – better clear the deck before I do anything else – thirty-two since this morning! New policies, regulations, directives. Scan Delete. Scan Delete. A meeting next week about St. Christina's Easter fund raiser. Scan Delete. Why can't a country that invented the space station's Canadarm figure out how to control its bureaucracies? A request for my staff's summer holiday roster. A telephone message, via Jacklyn, from Lucy's mother, an aged battle-axe who bears no physical resemblance to Lucy and insists that her daughter suffers from nothing more than a mild neurosis best cured by a naturopath. She wants me to call her. Uh oh. A report from Sergeant Gladnowitz.

'A spinning wheel with a 2 x 4 inch brass plaque nailed to the frame has been found in the living room of the Century stone house identified in C's break and entry charge information. The inscription is worn but can still be read:

Presented to Mrs. Neil MacIntyre
With Everlasting Gratitude,
By Captain Jonathan Prescott
On Behalf of

His Royal Highness George III
At the Town of Chester
In the year of Our Lord 1783
God Save The King.'

So C's story is true. The spinning wheel may be the reason for her crime.

'Present owners of the house say they acquired all contents with the house on 28/10/99. They have no knowledge of its history. Prior to their occupancy the house had stood vacant for three months following the death of its owner, a Miss D. MacIntyre, who died in Kempville Manor at the age of 93. Her estate was willed to a cousin in Manitoba who sold it with all its contents to the present owners.

Investigation continues on your other questions.'

I pull out Deirdre's story. Could it be true too? C says MacIntyre is not her name, but now I have a real family to explore. Are there more connections between Deirdre and my charge?

A bottle of Riesling, given to me last Christmas by a grateful patient's wife, resides in a mini fridge in the corner of my office. I keep forgetting to take it home and after the week I've had, don't I deserve a glass of wine? There is a corkscrew on the Swiss Army knife keychain the kids gave me for Christmas – I've never used it – and I have a china coffee mug. And at this hour who will see me having a drink while I read?

Jane Bow

Across the office, under the coat rack, my gym bag accuses – when was the last time I worked out? – but the prospect of going out into the dark, driving across town, getting changed, climbing onto a treadmill, pumping iron on a Friday night –

"Tomorrow." I tell it. There's an early Saturday morning aerobics class. "That's a promise."

Outside, above the river, clouds litter the darkening sky. My reflection in the window is a ghost, her body transparent, the river running through her as we raise our mugs to each other, then turn to C's diary.

... Neither Neil nor I had any idea what we were doing at first. We were so far from anything we knew, and there were trees to fell before we could plant anything; animals to track and trap or shoot, to hack to pieces in order to cure and store for meat; a house to build. But our closest neighbours, the Staedlers, who had spent twenty years in New England prior to coming north, showed us how to peel the bark off the logs, how to chink between them with moss, how to set a window frame, how to order from Halifax and then transport and finally mount a pane of glass.

It was not a perfect job, and the Nova Scotia winter nearly froze us that first year. Many were the mornings we'd wake up and find little mountains of snow piled inside the windowsill. Our turnips, potatoes, carrots ran out by Christmas, but though it was hard and our cabin was tiny, it was our own. There was plenty of fish and game and the neighbours showed us how to boil an Indian drink made of white cedar. We learned to make bread out of potatoes. Later we churned butter, made cheese, clothes, soap, candles, even moccasins. Stepping out of a life that did not fit us, we were making our own way, and how many people in this world ever have the freedom to do that?

I was a good spinner and weaver, with small, quick fingers. Before I came out here Neil's mother had given me her own spinning wheel to bring.

"When you touch this wheel, you'll be in touch with me," she told me, and sure enough it was true. On freezing evenings that first winter, when the sea wind was howling through the chinking between the logs, creeping in through all our woollens, right into our very bones, and the world outside was a howling darkness, I'd run my hand along that worn wheel and feel her strength flowing into me.

I began to make deals: a shawl for a month's supply of bread, a new linen shirt for the blacksmith paid for with a pound of nails.

Deirdre's vibrant and sexy marriage produced six babies: Pearl then Duncan, Joseph, Christy, Malcolm and Deirdre. Some died, some thrived. Meanwhile wealthy colonies to the south began to grumble about huge taxes the British kept levying.

In 1774, word came up with the traders from Boston that a crew of men dressed up as Indians had snuck onto a British supply ship in the night and dumped a whole load of British tea into Boston harbour, to protest. A year later, in 1775, farmers, tradespeople and politicians rallied behind makeshift barricades, fighting relentless lines of British redcoats with hunting rifles, stones and pitchforks.

Some gave up and came north, telling dreadful tales of civil chaos, hangings and mob lynchings.

Captain Prescott, governor of Chester, ordered all men to report to the blockhouse, in case the violence followed, and during the next five years Neil trained regularly with the militia. There wasn't a soul in town who would not lay down his or her life for gentle, understanding, intelligent Jonathan Prescott. When Pearl married Julian Bridges, a shipbuilder's son in the spring of 1780, he gave them a set of silverware, though a veil of apprehension hung over their wedding day. British soldiers were continuing to land in Boston and New York. To finance their resistance New England privateers had begun to sail north, raiding our towns, taking our livestock and guns, demanding money.

Three schooners arrived in Scotch Cove shortly after Pearl delivered our first granddaughter, in July, 1782. Did they know that all our men and older boys were out in the forest, chopping the town's winter supply of firewood? They must be planning to raid Chester!

I needed to warn Captain Prescott, and bring Pearl and her baby back here. Christy looked after little Malcolm and Deirdre while I ran along a path dappled with sunlight, the forest's trees rustling and dancing in an easterly wind taking the three ships towards Chester, their guns blasting already.

Cannonballs were falling like black snowballs out of hell when I reached Chester's blockhouse. Captain Prescott and a few militiamen – grandfathers too old to chop wood – were loading the town's cannon but the ships anchored around the end of Nass's Point, out of reach. It was nearly dark, the streets eerily silent when I hammered on Pearl's door.

Her sister-in-law Sarah, who helped with meals up at Captain Prescott's house, was already there. They had tipped Pearl's heavy oak table onto its side, a little pool of lantern light showing us dear new baby Deirdre in her cradle, and a musket on the floor behind it. Sarah took off her cloak and threw it over a chair.

Hundreds of men had landed, she said.

"And you never saw a nastier collection of evil-smelling louts, fat, muscle-bound hulks wearing torn black shirts or filthy leather jerkins; skinny, greasy, greedy-looking men in ponytails, carrying knives or flintlocks or muskets, and smirking."

Captain Prescott had invited the ships' captains to tea at the blockhouse, where they would tell him what he would have to give in order to keep his town safe. Sarah had served them.

"Once the privateer leaders were in the blockhouse eating and drinking, their men back on their ships, Captain Prescott had his son John deliver a note to him. 'Gentlemen,' he told them, 'I feel it is only fair to warn you that a regiment of the King's men has been apprised of our plight and is heading this way.'"

A bluff. To buy us one night, and half of tomorrow at most.

"Let me light a tiny fire," said Sarah, "Just enough to heat some water and make tea."

Firelight picked out the bright lining of her cloak. I had used a bolt of red cotton from Virginia to make it, along with a dozen others just like it. It gave me such an idea.

Captain Prescott was sitting in his study signing papers when Sarah and I arrived. He looked so tired. I had Sarah put on her cloak inside out.

"You know how the telescope distorts with distance, Captain, and in the light of dawn. And these hooligans are expecting to see redcoats."

He sat there for the longest time, looking at the top of his desk, then finally stood up, turned Sarah this way and that.

Next morning, before the sun shot its first rays into our bay, all of Chester's able-bodied women hid their little ones under overturned rain barrels, in root cellars, in the woods with their grandmothers. Then, broomsticks slung over our shoulders, we climbed the hill to the blockhouse wearing our cloaks inside out. What a motley crew, our broomsticks shaking. Someone giggled.

Shh!" hissed someone else. "Sound travels on the water!"

"I will be issuing soldier commands," Captain Prescott told us, "but you need not pay any heed. Just keep on marching back and forth."

First light turned the sea to pewter grey. The ships came from between the point and Gooseberry Island, their sails set to a cross wind though the bay was still as a mirror. As soon as they reached the lee of the island, their canvas luffed.

And I don't think in all my years I have ever known the sweating, knee-rattling, head pounding terror of what became a sunny July morning: marching, trying to make one foot follow the other, back straight, chin up, watching and waiting with no way of knowing whether the pirates were close enough to see us clearly. But we kept on marching. Another hour passed and another, and still they did not lower their dinghies. Finally, around noon, the wind came up.

Captain Prescott bellowed another order, then took out his telescope.

"They're turning tail, but keep marching!"

We waited until they had tacked away out to sea and then oh! If they had looked back they would have seen redcoats hugging and kissing each other, all of us weeping with such joy and relief and oh, what a triumph!

A year later Chester celebrated the end of that revolution with a military band and speeches in the main square. One of the presentations was to me, a beautiful little spinning wheel, made of maple. Nailed to the frame was a shiny brass plaque:

> *Presented to Mrs. Neil MacIntyre*
> *With the Everlasting Gratitude of*
> *Captain Jonathan Prescott On Behalf of*
> *His Royal Highness George III*
> *At the Town of Chester*
> *In the year of Our Lord 1783*
> *God Save The King.*

Feet up on the open bottom drawer of my desk, I return to the present. Raise my coffee mug in a toast.

"To you, Deirdre, an unknown Canadian heroine – Why don't I know your story, why don't we all? – and to you, C, for writing this beautiful piece of history."

Outside, night has descended. The birds have gone to bed. My reflection takes another mouthful of wine and raises a see-through eyebrow.

You too come from people who left everything they knew in Scotland to start a new life here, Dr. Dumbnuts. And what do you know about them, or about any of your family's history, past Grandma and Grandpa? Zilch, that's what. Nobody told stories in my family. What happened in the Old World could stay in the Old World.

Some primitive people believe stories spring out of the landscape we call home, that humans are merely their tellers. Is that what happened to C, she just heard the story and wrote it down?

No. Too facile. Choices make us who we are. And no one takes the care necessary to write like C unless they are trying to do, or know something. I drink some more wine.

… Stepping out of a life that did not fit us, we were making our own way, and how many people in this world ever have the freedom to do that?

You got that right, C. Who has freedom any time anywhere? And why is my mug nearly empty? The wine bottle is a dead soldier. How did that happen? My reflection is wobbling around the edges. Usually we wear our fly-away, mousy, once-upon-a-time blond hair swept up into a bun that takes no time in the morning, and goes with any suit. Now however, great clumps of it have escaped the elastic, hanging down over one ear, the other eye. A smudge of mascara under the visible eye gives away the fact that we have shed a tear or two.

"Well whaddaya know, Twinkle Toes?"

Yeah, what do I know? Bugger all, that's what. We psychologists create theories and models and then lay them over people's behaviour but really, what does any of it have to do with real, trying living and dying? Guess where dear old Freud got a lot of his ideas. From Shakespeare: Macbeth on guilt and conscience, Lear on familial love and ego break-down; the list goes on. And then there was Jung, whose great leap in understanding the role of mythological archetypes within the human psyche came during a psychotic episode, unexamined by reason's rigours. Also – my reflection and I look at each other – face it girlfriend, a lot of what we learned in school is obsolete already. Functional MRIs tracking chemistry in the working brain are finding new neurological connections every week, but what does it all add up to? Guesswork, the brain a miraculous sack of neurons and dendrites and chemicals beyond its own capacity of comprehend.

"Ha." I like that, am draining my mug in a toast to guesswork when St. Christina's fire alarm starts ringing. I jump up. My foot catches the edge of the open desk drawer.

"Steady, girl," says my reflection. Someone trying to sneak out for a smoke probably opened the wrong door. The alarm bell goes on clamouring. Please someone, turn it off.

No one does. Better pay attention, check on my unit. First, put wine bottle and mug in drawer. Tuck hair behind ears. Lick a finger, rub off my mascara tears. Stand tall. My lips cheeks forehead feel wooden. My reflection makes faces, trying to loosen them.

"You okay Dr. Pumps?" Voice sounds fine. "One step at a time."

Maria and Lucy are in the hallway outside C's room.

"Bitch!" says Maria. Lucy giggles.

The men are grouped like sheep a little way down the hall. All except Stan.

"It's C, boss," chimes Radio. "C and Stan, C and Stan, C and –"

"Okay Radio," Mike puts a hand on his shoulder. I am not sure I can bear to look.

Six-foot three-inch Stan is splayed out on C's bedroom floor, one booted leg under her bed, loose white flesh on his belly peeking out where his shirt has hiked up. His face under its stubble looks pale, flaccid, a picture of shabby, barely conscious forty two year-old pathos. Steve and a new staff member – Ross? Ray? – kneel, one on each side of him, Steve trying to hold a blood-soaked cloth against the side of Stan's head just above his right ear. Stan keeps jerking his head away, his eyes, usually slightly derisive, rolling like a shot deer's.

"Easy, man." Blood pooling on the floor runs into the knee of Steve's khaki uniform pants.

He's alive at least. Head wounds usually look worse than they are. I kneel next to Ross/Ray, pray he does not smell wine, and lift Stan's beefy wrist to take his pulse. The grey safari shirt he lives in reeks of old sweat. He blinks at me, ruining my count. Oh well, the pulse is strong and steady.

"Get her outta here Doc," his words are a whisper, slurring, "shedon'tbelong ..." His eyes close.

"Stay awake, Stan." My voice sounds loud, piercing. The wound, when I peek under the cloth, oozes purple, showing bone.

How the hell did he get in here?

C is still holding the leg of the chair with which, presumably, she did the damage and then tried to punch a hole in her wire meshed window, triggering the alarm. Is that why she did it? The curtain of her hair is closed but I can hear harsh intakes of breath. The bomber jacket is on the bed, the top buttons of her Faith Hill blouse unbuttoned. Was she getting ready for bed when he came in? Why didn't the goddamn camera catch him? And why didn't she start yelling? Someone would have come. How close to her did the brute get before she hefted the chair and swung it? An earthquake of repercussions will follow this, but how the hell am I supposed to tame this monster of a man without the use of a black hole, an oubliette in which to conveniently *oublier* him?

Rosa bustles into the room. "Come with me, C girl."

C turns away. I get to my feet but do not go near her. Lucy is watching through the doorway, her eyes trained on Stan. God alone knows what her brain's addled cells are conjuring. I tell Ross/Ray to remove the rest of the PMIs from the hall. Two nurses and the hospital's doctor on call arrive with a stretcher. I watch them load Stan, taking long slow breaths, the kind I model for Normie, and turn to

Steve.

"Stay beside him all night. The doctor will have you wake him every hour. You," I tell C, "I will deal with on Monday."

A cab drives me home. Ernie's Audi is parked in the driveway.

What's happened? Panic slips my leash: it's 9:37 pm. Why hasn't he called me?

News of a flexible brush for scrubbing toilet bowls is blaring out of the television. Sitting wide-eyed in front of it is Kay. The program switches back to The Bachelorette. Horrified, I sit down beside her, catch her little girl scents of crayon and Cheerios and toothpaste.

"Sweetheart?" I flick the remote's Off button.

"Mom!" Rage in the nightie we bought last fall, too short in sleeves and length already. When did her pudgy little arms and legs become so long and thin? "Daddy said I could watch!"

Her anger ignites my own. I clamp it down.

"Where is Daddy?"

"Downstairs in his study." Chin jutting, quavering, eyes exhausted. "And he said –!"

Correction: in what used to be his study.

"Where's Normie?"

She glares and right away I know. A tantrum, refusal to leave probably, Normie bawling, Ernie trying to force him, and poor little Kay watching, helpless.

I wrap my arms around her. Normie must be

asleep now.

My special English-muffin-with-cream-cheese-and-maple-syrup snack dribbles onto Kay's wrists, bringing a tiny grin. I tuck her into bed, stroke her back. Wish I could crawl in beside her.

When I come downstairs Ernie is hovering in the kitchen doorway, his coat on, laptop bag over his shoulder. His face is grey with fatigue, his brown eyes empty of emotion.

"I told her she could wait up for you."

"She's seven years old, Ernie. Couldn't you leave your goddamn computer long enough to read to her, cuddle her?"

"You think I didn't try?"

"Not enough, obviously."

"If they hadn't been basket cases when I got here. Do you always come home at 10 pm?"

I want to hit him. How does he know I was at work tonight, with yet another crisis? Maybe I was out on a Friday night date, luxuriating in my freedom, or a new passion. Somewhere behind my solar plexus a tsunami threatens.

"Look Ernie, I don't mind you bringing them here instead of taking them away on your weekend, but wouldn't it be great if, when I get home, I could find a little calm?" I turn away, take a tissue from a box on the kitchen counter and blow my nose, trying to stem the tidal wave.

His car growls out of the driveway. A hum from the furnace clicks off. Leaving me with nothing but steady dripping from the kitchen faucet. And the lurking question:

Is he right? Mothers are instrumental in setting up the psychologic frameworks through which their children come to know life. I love Kay and little Normie more than life itself but how can I show them that when I'm only with them for an hour or two at either end of a long, trouble-ridden day? A sob comes loose.

There is no one to hear it and I am too worn out and wobbly to keep myself from giving in, riding the heaving wave inside which a whole school of questions flicker with life: about my mothering, my choice of job, about Ernie's and my sex life, such as it was, and my performance at work. One of my charges is in hospital with a hole in his head, his attacker traumatized, a hospital window broken.

Face it Dr. Tutti Frutti, you're a loser. Try try try, that's all you ever do, but my my my, what a mess you brew. An F on every count: a fucking forlorn female fruitcake of a failure, that's you. My tears flow freely.

"So what, Dr. Swat?" The voice I hear belongs to C. "If you don't think you measure up, why don't you quit?"

"Quit what?" Being a psychologist? A Mom? I have already quit being a wife. I rest my head against the back of my chair, tears dripping. Should I have walked away from ten years of training to spend my days baking cookies, playing games, painting a mural along the back fence, coaxing ivy, wisteria, purple clematis to grow up around it? Making certain my children knew their mother was there for them every minute of every day? Sadness sits like a stone in the bottom of my stomach.

* * *

Sunday night: the children are in bed. The stapler that has been clamping my brain ever since my drinking binge has loosened but my head and stomach are still fragile. I make myself a cup of ginger tea and open my laptop. Must find a way to get C out of the forensic unit, and out of my life. Making notes always helps:

Initial comparisons of C's and Deirdre's stories

- In both stories the women are creative shapers of events. C goes beyond the restraint of the law. Deirdre did not hesitate to transgress beyond restraints of family and custom.
- C loves David, a big man. Deirdre loved Neil, a big man.
- C writes and talks a lot about sex and orgasms.

... I stretched, smiling, under the blanket. I was a brand new edition of myself, pink and glistening, all my sharp angles turned into lovely curves, my every move so graceful ...

When have I ever stretched, pink and

glistening –?

Stop it, Elaine. Go to bed.

Ernie must have given the children Cheerios for dinner on Friday. Monday morning there is enough left in the box for one bowlful so, rather than trying to facilitate sibling negotiations, I dump pancake mix usually reserved for weekends into a bowl, trying to ignore the stone still lodged in the pit of my stomach.

Kay comes into the kitchen dressed in a combination of ballet leotard and new peddle-pushers I bought at a Boxing Day sale, even though the temperature outside is below zero. Seeing the pancake mix, she claps her hands.

Normie bangs his spoon on the table.

"Treat! Treat! Treat!" A new headache threatens me.

"Shshsh, honey." I hand him a segment of orange. "Kay, go up and put on jeans, socks and a sweater."

"Mummyyy!"

"Now."

And she does. Normie looks at me as if I am not to be trusted. Can I blame him?

Five

Florescent tube lights in my office ceiling give off a
dead white glare that goes straight to my headache.
Outside, the black streak down the middle of the St.
Lawrence River has widened but dark clouds banked
above it are sagging – a late snow storm? Jacklyn has
turned on our coffee maker, thank God.

Stan is fine, stitched up and re-installed in his
own bed, but any minute now my phone will begin
to ring with doctors, lawyers, the hospital's chief of
staff, Sergeant Gladnowitz wanting to discuss the
laying of charges. Against whom?

If Stan is charged with sexual assault and
I find him criminally responsible and fit to stand
trial he will be convicted and off my hands for the
duration of his prison sentence. I will be able to
concentrate on the others, maybe even try out some
new rehabilitation ideas. But where is the evidence
against Stan? The unit's video tape shows him walking
towards C's room wearing a silly smirk, opening her
door. Breaking the cardinal 'No Bedroom Visits'
rule. Expecting, probably, to have a little fun before
the orderlies arrive. The camera inside the bedroom,
above the door, shows C standing by her bed, facing
away from it, unbuttoning her blouse presumably.
Startled, then alarmed, she turns. Picks up the chair
beside her bed. What happened next? What did Stan
say or do? Safe in the blind spot just inside the door,

he is not visible as she moves towards him, wielding the chair like a lion tamer. Did he touch her before she clobbered him? There's no video evidence.

As for C, facing a psychopathic rapist in her bedroom, how could she do anything but react? Yet if she is found to be 'criminally responsible' in that moment and is charged with assault, in the absence of any evidence of crime on Stan's part, she could be convicted. How brutal, cruel and unfair would that be? I have got to get her out of here.

Forty seven emails await me. Forty seven since Friday night! I hit Select All. My finger hovers over Delete, but I chicken out, stab Exit instead. A new 'C' tape is lying on my desk. Maybe it will help me understand her part in what happened last night. It is blank. I rewind, play it again. Silence.

A broken recorder, or is C toying with me? Is she nothing more than an enraged female? Are Deirdre, the spinning wheel story, the bridge and David all fabrications built by an imaginative mind gone wild? Whatever the case, her anger is nothing compared to mine this morning.

My laptop beeps, a new email from Sergeant Gladnowitz:

'1. Computer referencing of unsolved missing persons reports across Canada over the last two years, focussing on educated females aged 25-34 who have brown hair and blue eyes yielded 13 possibilities. Of these one was last seen driving a silver Mustang. Name: Cailey Armstrong; age 29; address: 4193 Carling Avenue, Ottawa. A cross-Canada computer check under this name has yielded no matches.'

C is for Cailey. Gotcha!

'2.   A woman did pay $1200 for a blue Holt Renfrew dress and matching shoes in December.
    The saleswoman remembers her because cash transactions of this magnitude are
    rare and the woman was so scruffy.
'3.   Several homeless men known to Toronto police are named David. We will pick them up,
    question them, but I am not optimistic about useful results.'

Never mind, I have a name: the treasured key with which to snap open this case. I may be a professional but here in the privacy of my office my anger turns into a fist pump. I pour myself a second cup of coffee, ask Jacklyn to have C brought to me.

"My staff tells me you spent hours this weekend making a second tape, Cailey Armstrong."

Hearing her name, she startles, shows fear. She did not sleep much over the weekend and the staff says the other PMIs keep a few feet of space between them and her, evidently preferring the bully they know to this unknown lunatic.

"And then you erased it."

"Whatever you say, Dr. Feet-of-Clay."

"Why?"

Her bomber jacket shoulders shrug.

I have off-loaded the care of my four-year old and his sweet seven-year old sister for this? I picture myself coming to my feet, leaning across the desk –

She watches me, her face blank as a rabbit's.

Get hold of yourself. I take my time opening her file, remind myself that twenty-three severely disturbed residents who have to call this hospital home need all the energy I can muster, and fix her with a look in which there is nothing but business.

"Look Cailey Armstrong, here's where we are this morning. If you admit to your name and tell me exactly, truthfully, what happened last night, and also what made you decide to break the laws that have landed you in my unit, I will do my best to help you. Because the police will investigate –"

"What happened was self-defence! The surveillance tape will show –"

"What?" My voice slices across hers. "That a woman who breaks into houses, who refuses to give her name, is also violent enough to beat a heavily drugged man. You could go to prison, Cailey. Very few arch-criminals are toiling behind bars, most are poor pathetic miscreants caught up as one sorry set of circumstances builds on another. Like you."

She looks down at her bruised hand, flexes her fingers, weighing her choices. Realizes she has none. I click on my phone recorder and push it across the desk towards her.

"Now, Cailey Armstrong: is that your name?"

"Yes."

I consult the police report.

"Most recently of 4193 Carling Avenue, Ottawa?"

"No."

I wait.

"What I told you about driving to Nova Scotia and Deirdre and David, living in the ravine, all of that is true." She watches a chickadee feeding outside the window.

"And your family, your sister, where is she?"

"There is no sister. I made her up to put you off."

"You made her up." The eyes I train on her are nails I will hammer into her warm body if necessary. "It's time to stop fooling with me, Cailey."

"I know, I know," she sits up straight. Her features settle into what might possibly be resigned relief. I sit back, letting the feeling sink in.

"Why don't you just start talking. Who are you?"

"Who was I before? A nameless, faceless government functionary, that's who, a GF. Note the lack of a vowel in the acronym because vowels are the breath of life and up there on the fifteenth floor windows were sealed as we GF's scurried from meeting to computer to meeting setting objectives, developing 'policies and procedures,' writing hundred-page reports nobody read. Do you know the definition of evil, Doc? Action without accountability or morality – a perfect description of a government bureaucracy." Her blue eyes scrutinize me. "But my guess is that you know that."

"So why didn't you quit? You are obviously educated."

Her ragged eyebrows arc derisively.

"To do what? Work for some corporation making junk nobody needs? Or selling it, getting people to buy buy buy –"

"There must be jobs you could do. But no, you chose to drive away. Why?"

She stares at her fingernails. I wait. When she looks up I see despair.

"I don't honestly know."

"Where were you living?"

"With a partner – smart, good looking, excellent prospects, lots of mutual interests – in a high rise condo, screwing regularly, buying coffee at Starbucks, having dinner parties. What more could a woman possibly want, right?" Her laugh sounds like twisting metal.

"What about your parents?"

"My father is an elite GF, my mother an American lawyer who lasted in government just long enough for me to grow up, then went back to New York."

"Are you in touch?"

"We used to text back and forth, but she's

always pretty busy."

"What about friends? You must have some?"

"Sure, hundreds, on Facebook, Twitter, Instagram. Guess how many noticed when I left."

"Tell me about that, the actual decision to leave."

Her bomber jacket shoulders rise again.

"It wasn't a decision. I stopped on the way home to buy detergent, and when I got back into the car I just kept on driving, up the ramp onto the highway. Mustangs are such great cars, Doc: stick shift, so smooth, and black leather upholstery, four speaker surround sound. So I just kept on going. When the highway divided – north, south or east – I turned east, pressed the pedal to the metal because I had a few dollars in my wallet, a phone card, and for everything else there's Master Card, right? And singing along with my playlist, there was this wonderful, fuck-you sense of euphoria. So I kept on driving –"

"With no plan?"

"None. After two days and a night, I came to a beach on the south shore of Nova Scotia: wild waves booming onto log-strewn sand, no people at the end of April. There was a rug in the car so I parked and got out and just sat, wrapped in my blanket, watching the waves until a crescent moon came up in such a cold blue-black sky, feeling the waves rolling in, breaking with a bang, unfurling across the sand."

"And then?"

"I must have slept. By the time the first rays lit the morning horizon my blanket, my hair, my cheeks, were covered in salt water pearls. My knees, ankles, neck were stiff with cold. I found some cardboard coffee at a gas station and drove north along the coast. And found Chester. Remembered my mother telling me once that my ancestors first settled there. So I turned in, to look them up in the township archives. Their original house was a log cabin at Scotch Cove."

A trace of enthusiasm? She is gazing out the window, into memory.

"The cabin's dirt floor was strewn with hoe handles, rusty axes, a bedstead, an old engine. A fireplace built into the back wall was falling apart but its stones were black with my ancestors' soot. It was a large cabin, with a loft, and there was light up there. Ladder rungs built onto the side wall creaked as I climbed them. The fourth one snapped under my weight so I laid an old wooden stepladder against the rotten rungs, and then I was climbing up through cobwebs and dust motes shining silver in sunlight coming through a little window. Beside it was an old ladder back rocking chair, its wicker seat a frayed hole. And a trunk." Cailey glances at me. Sometime during her discourse she has slipped off David's bomber jacket. No other discernible change has taken place but now the woman on the other side of my desk bears little resemblance to furtive, sassy, shut-down 'C.' Telling her story has softened her eyes and the set of her jaw above her Faith Hill shirt. "And it was as if the loft had been waiting all these years for me, was breathing with me. The trunk's pigskin lid was green with mould but I could trace the remains of initials embossed on it: D.M. Inside there were pictures, some lying loose, others mounted in a mouldy leather album, much newer than the cabin. Underneath them was a painting of a young couple, very old, the lines and colours faded nearly away in places, the heavy parchment yellow, crumbling around the edges. I lifted it out of the trunk. The man was much taller than the woman, large boned with light-coloured eyes and bushy black hair, wearing an army red coat, tartan kilt and blue bonnet. The woman was a little bird. Calligraphy at the bottom of the painting named them: Deirdre and Neil McIntyre, 1762. And there was this spark between them, as if the moment the artist finished they would close together." She stops. I wait.

"You're not going to understand, Doc. You've never heard the voice of a dead person."

"Give me another chance." She hesitates.

"Okay then, it's all in the catch phrases, little ups and downs of pitch that are distinct. You can not doubt that the person is with you." My incredulity betrays me. Her tone sharpens, becomes that of a woman who would not hesitate to break a chair over a man's head. "Tell you what Dr. Diehard, turn off your single-track scientific looney bin doctor mind and think of it this way: our bodies are made of cells.

But what are cells? A collections of molecules made of atoms clumped together, and what are atoms? Electrons orbiting nuclei, quanta: energy. And you know that energy never dies. So, if everything is energy, why can't we summon a person by collecting their energy in our minds in the same way that your recorder is collecting the energy that is my voice?"

Jacklyn knocks. The hospital's chief of staff is with the police and wants to see me. Good. I am in no mood for a discussion of metaphysics, and dropping her armour, facing herself, has left Cailey pale with fatigue. I will check on my other PMI/criminal first, and we will finish this later today.

* * *

We have allowed Stan to spend the morning in bed to cover ourselves medically and, in all honesty, to keep him from making everyone's life miserable. I find him sitting up, wearing flannel pyjamas so ancient the coloured pattern has nearly faded away, one of his roommate Jeffrey Day's car magazines on his lap. Jeffrey's half of the room is partitioned by a floor to ceiling bookcase in which he keeps his magazines, a sound system, the video game machine he hooks up to a small monitor: such is the home of a long-term PMI. A gifted mechanic, Jeffrey spends his days under a car in a garage downtown. We drop him off in the morning, pick him up after work. As long as he takes his medication he is fully functional – one of our success stories. Stan has the side of the room with a window that looks out at the parking lot and a snow-covered knoll behind it.

"My head hurts, Doc." Petulant as a schoolboy.

"What were you doing in a female patient's room, Stan?"

He glowers, does not want to vacate the cozy role of invalid.

"She's nuts, Doc, a danger to us all."

"So why didn't you stay away from her?"

Lucy comes into the hall as I am leaving Stan's room, red lipstick smeared in the general vicinity of her lips. She is supposed to be painting ceramic Easter bunnies with the others.

"Is he all right, Dr. Price? Can I visit him?" A snicker escapes her.

"Lucy!" Julie, our newest staff member, hurries out of the craft room. "That's not the way to the washroom." Gingerly, she takes hold of her charge's toothpick arm. Lucy jerks away, still looking at me.

I raise a schoolmistress-like eyebrow. I am a juggler trying, day after day, not to drop balls so heavy they will break someone's foot.

* * *

The storm clouds have dropped their load and left the outside world pristine white under a weak sun sliding down now behind the frozen St. Lawrence. Taking her place on the other side of my desk, Cailey seems calm, sane.

"You met Deirdre in Nova Scotia, then ran out of gas, sold your car, and took a bus to Toronto. What happened next? How did you come to be wearing a Holt Renfrew dress?"

She looks sheepish.

"Suddenly there I am downtown, on Bloor Street, Christmas lights and decorations everywhere as if we're all one big holly-jolly Jesus-worshipping family, except that everybody's hurry hurry hurrying, all black leather, pointed shoes, strained faces, bags of booze. Holt Renfrew was right there and I was cold so I went in. And this anorexic, Sassoon-sculpted forty-something saleslady looked down her nose at me – I may have looked a little grubby – so I picked up a $340 bottle of eau de cologne. "I'll take that." Then of course I needed a dress to go with it. When I got to the top of the escalator the dress department manager actually wrinkled her nose. So I started trying on ball gowns, turning this way and that in front of the mirror, imagining myself on the red carpet at the Oscars and, I have to admit, enjoying the annoyance of the manager and her other dress-buying customers. The beautiful royal blue cocktail dress I finally chose, to match my eyes, cost $1200. Then I had to get shoes –"

"And you were thinking?"

"No," she shakes her head, "not thinking."

"Was your friend Deirdre with you during all this?"

Cailey stops, looks confused, a little threatened?

"You know," I smile, "the way she's with you in here?"

No reply.

"So, you're beautifully dressed now. What did you do next?"

"What was there left for me to do? It was dark, cold, I knew no one, so I took myself out for a slap-up dinner – east coast lobster, the finest Pouilly-Fuissé – then hailed a cab and had the driver drop me at the Bloor Street Viaduct. Gave him what was left of my Mustang money. Why not?"

"And Deirdre? What did she think of all this?"

Cailey breathes through her nose, noisily, clearly annoyed. She does not know.

"That stupid wire thing they've built outside the bridge railings, to get us suicides to go somewhere less public, what a joke that is. All you have to do is climb out around the end and work your way along until you're above the parkway underneath."

"But you didn't jump." I watch her remember why we are here, trying to gauge what will happen next. "Thanks to David."

No response.

Disaffection at work could make a person flee. Bureaucracies are soul-gobbling nightmares within which there is no salvation … but suicide? Something is missing from this story. I flip back through the transcript of her tape recording, stop at her description of the man who saved her.

"'A hug from him is a place to get lost in ...' and 'he built me my life …'" I look up. "Sounds like quite a guy. I'd like to meet him."

She gives me a wan, deeply sad, that's-never-going-to-happen smile.

"Please Doc, don't make me lose him."

* * *

We stop at the zoo on the way home. It's feeding time, I see the sign every day, but today I turn into the parking lot. It's Ernie's and my ninth anniversary, does that have anything to do with why? We have always dined at Chez Henri, a riverside restaurant just outside of town, even though April is tax season, Ernie's busiest time of year. Henri, who grew up in Montreal, would call us by name, greeting us with the same joke every year:

"*Sacré coeur*, you two are still married?"

This year the answer seems to be no. Remembering last weekend makes me feel like crying. Ernie has not called since. So get over it, Elaine. Stop pining for something that no longer exists.

"Come on," I tell the children, "let's watch the muskrats have dinner."

"I have to go to piano."

I look at Kay in the rearview mirror. She looks so grown-up in a seat belt instead of her car seat.

"Do you want to go to piano?"

"No, she doesn't!" Normie shouts from his car seat beside her. "Kay hates piano! Let's go see the muskrats, Mom, and the monkeys!"

Kay stares into her lap, desire fighting with righteous petulance.

Please God don't let her leave delicious, spontaneous early childhood behind just yet, before I've had time ... Or is this a little girl's rebellion against always living in the shadow thrown by her little brother's need, growing up in a house where days have to be rigidly ordered, where distress blows up without warning. Poor child, I reach back to squeeze her hand.

"Let's do it, just this once, just for a minute." Fear stretches my smile.

Inside his pool one of the muskrats looks at us, then swims along the glass, glancing over his shoulder. Shrieking with glee, Normie pulls away from me to chase him. The muskrat steps on the gas, reaches the end of the enclosure, looks at Normie, then swims back, Normie clomping along in his snow boots, hard on his tail. I glance at Kay in time to glimpse a hint of a smile, and give thanks.

Too tired, after the dinner dishes are done, to face making tomorrow's lunches, I enlist Kay's help.

"You can make yourself whatever you want."

"Really?" She reaches for the peanut butter and jelly, eying me suspiciously then, when I do nothing but smile, sets to work making a roll-up. "Do we have any toothpicks?"

So of course Normie wants a roll-up too. A four-year old making his own lunch? Tonight I don't care. Fingers and faces smeared with raspberry jelly, the kids look happy.

I am still up at midnight, sitting in my recliner, sipping red wine and thinking about Cailey's story, making notes:

- Deirdre and Cailey share the same energy, of course they do. One is a fabrication of the other and this can help me. What each of us sees, hears, smells, feels and knows is an inextricable mesh of what is there and who we are, our brains sieving every incoming message through our experiences/biases/perspectives/proclivities. Tell a wine expert he/she is drinking plonk and he/she will criticize it. Tell him/her the same wine is a Chateau Lafitte Rothschild and he/she will wax eloquently about body, bouquet and the taste of sunlight. We all do the same.
- Finding Deirdre and bringing her heroism to life gave Cailey an escape from suicidal meaninglessness, but escapes cannot not hold up against dark, lonely homelessness on a cold winter night.

• David saved her with love, and gave Cailey
the strength to find her ancestors' stone house,
and with it a way to connect with a past that
felt meaningful. Other cultures, believing our
ancestors' spirits are with us, would call Cailey
a sensitive, would revere her vision. Would not
label her delusional or a criminal.

The telephone rings. Dear God, what now?
Can I not have one quiet evening –?

"Lainie? I'm sorry to be calling so late."
Ernie.

"Are you all right?" His voice sounds as if
it's only getting half the air it needs.

"Yeah ... I was just thinking, it being our
anniversary ..." He wants to talk. Will I meet him
tomorrow night for dinner at Chez Henri?

Who knew my body's juices were so close
to the surface? Hanging up, I feel jittery as a virgin.

Six

By the time I drive the children home after Normie's skating lesson heavy clouds are once again blocking the sun. I have spent all day reviewing Cailey's case, instructing Jacklyn to cancel my appointments and take telephone messages so that I could reach a conclusion, write my assessment report, and then celebrate by having dinner with my husband.

Cailey is fit to stand trial. She was also in clear possession of her faculties when she climbed into that century home. But was she 'criminally responsible?' How does a person who feels that her life has added up to zero, that nothing she thinks, feels or says has ever made any difference to anyone, apply concepts of 'right' and 'wrong'? Cailey would insist that breaking into that particular house was not wrong. Does that suggest mental illness? The woman who drove out of her life, and found first Deirdre then David, and love, real, giving, enduring love in a ravine does not fit any profile I know. "Please Doc, don't make me lose him." How can I do that, wrestle this misguided young woman out of the tentacles of a system that will destroy her no matter what I decide? Hustling the children in to Amanda, I am no closer to an answer than I was when I left the house this morning.

I spend an hour stewing over what to wear. Why? It's not as if we have a sexy marriage, or any kind of marriage, but at least he wants to talk. I settle on a simple black dress, the single pearl Ernie gave me on our anniversary last year and my new red knee-high boots. Seeing myself in the front hall mirror, I feel a whisper of something that might be hope. There was a reason, after all, that I married this man and had children with him. He will meet me at the restaurant.

Damp wind buffets the car as I drive down the St. Lawrence parkway. A storm is blowing in, warns the radio. Never mind, Chez Henri is a cozy nest of candle-lit tables, murmured conversations punctuated by the occasional ripple of laughter. A fire crackles in a central hearth.

Ernie is not here yet. The maître d' shows me to a table for two and leaves me with a liquor menu of cocktails you have to be wearing a Marilyn Munroe dress to order: frothy pink Bellinis, orange Screwdrivers, lime green Lady Manhattans, red-to-orange Tequila Sunrises, hundreds of sugar and alcohol calories in a single glass and I haven't been to the gym all week.

He stands in the doorway peeling off his gloves finger by finger as he scans the hubbub of diners. Outside it must have started snowing. Crystals glimmer for a moment before melting into the spiky thickness of his hair. He sees me finally and crosses towards me, not smiling. He has driven all the way out here from the city, is that why? Or does he want to apologize for last weekend? Salt and pepper has begun to tinge his gold-red sideburns, I had not noticed that. As he reaches the table I see new lines at the edges of his mouth, his eyes.

The waiter is a twenty-something with pointy-head hair.

"Will you have a drink to start?"

"Yes please. I'll have a Sex on the Beach." I blush, but why not? Set a new tone.

"And you, sir?'

"Scotch on the rocks." Ernie leans back in his chair, relaxing. "How was Normie's lesson?" I am pleased that he has remembered.

"He still cries when they won't let him go flying around the rink." Danger zone: Shut up, Elaine. "But he is only four –"

"And so athletic. He could play on an advanced hockey team next year."

God help us. Helmeted hockey tots scrabbling after the puck, their five-year old faces hidden behind wire mesh protectors, Mom/Dad up in the stands sipping cardboard coffee, yelling like banshees, Normie needs that like he needs a dentist's drill.

Ernie's attention turns to the menu. I follow his lead, running my eyes down the list of entrees, eliminating out of habit – too much saturated animal fat, too rich, too heavy – and mentally questioning: is the pickerel fresh, is the crab meat real, how many kilometres will I have to run on the treadmill tomorrow?

My Sex on the Beach arrives, complete

with pink pleated-paper umbrella. Ernie cocks an eyebrow. I close my menu. I want to reach across the table and take his hand, divert his attention to the pearl at my throat, that he gave me right here, "a pearl of wisdom," he said then, "created out of friction, through endurance." This man has loved me, been loved by me. We know each other deeply. I picture us returning to the house, turning on the family room fire, something slow and blue on the stereo as excruciatingly slowly he undoes the buttons of my blouse. There is a faux fur rug on the floor: *the feel of him inside of me so sweet and urgent –*

The waiter returns, pen poised.

"I'll have the filet mignon please, rare."

Ernie orders fish.

I am halfway through my steak, roasted baby potatoes, crisp green beans, carrot spears decoratively splashed with a cream sauce – a still life on a plate – and wondering whether to order a second glass of Folonari Classico. We have not traded more than a few phrases. Is Ernie watching the same internal movie I am? He looks up, feeling my gaze?

"How's your dinner?" I smile.

"Delicious." His pan fried pickerel eyes me deadly. "Yours?"

"Good."

He goes back to eating, methodically cutting each bite to the same size, then stops.

"I wanted to talk to you, Elaine."

"Right." I smile again.

"You don't pay attention to these things but the fact is serious economic trouble is brewing. Everyone thinks the 2008 meltdown can't happen again but what I'm seeing –"

The faux fur rug disappears. A squall of disappointment blows through me.

"You invited me to Chez Henri to talk finances?" My tongue feels like sandpaper.

Annoyance, nothing else, crosses his face and I am crushed, exhausted suddenly. What was I thinking? Why would we suddenly, magically leave behind who we really are? My hand empties my wine glass into my mouth. My feet find purchase, push back my chair.

Ernie watches impassively as I pick up my purse, probably thinking I am on my way to the powder room. I cross the dining room, push open the doors into the vestibule, put on my coat and go out into the night.

The wind has died. Snow is falling silently, swirling up on currents of warmth that have escaped the restaurant with me. The storm has already put white hats on the lanterns outside the restaurant's front door. My red boots print footsteps in the glistening parking lot. Flakes land in my hair, on my eyelashes as I pass my car, steak and wine and Sex on thea Beach powering me up a little rise towards darkness and the highway. To cross a line, leave guilt and obligation, duty and justification, all of it behind. I do not look back.

Which way?

Right, east, away, following the river –

No. Because here in my mind is Kay, her seven-year old eyes confused.

"Mom's gone? Where?" Panic. "Why?"

Ernie has not come after me. Damn him, has he even noticed my absence? Or is he paying the bill now, putting on his coat? My turn to panic. Am I creating this scene to blow open what we are, and are not? No, I am running, afraid of a finality from which there can be no return. I dig into my pocket, find my car's remote key, hear its engine purrs into life, its headlights winking as I slither back down into the parking lot, slam my car door and gun the engine.

Snow has blanketed the river parkway, it's hard to see the edges of the road in my headlights, but the hospital is only a couple of kilometres away and there is a bedroom there for doctors on call or patients' family members on emergency visits. I park in the main lot and go in through the hospital's front door. No need for the forensic unit staff to know about my failed marriage.

My office desk lamp casts a homey circle of light. I tip my chair back, put my boots up on the desk. Such beautiful boots. Noticed by me, only me. Psychologist, expert on how the patterns of human nature play out, I live in a vacuum. Except for my children. I pick up the phone, ask if Amanda can stay the night, and warn her that Ernie might show up, though I doubt it.

My laptop is right in front of me, Cailey's assessment report still unwritten, but how to lose myself in work with this stomach full of slimy, wriggling, food-fat anger?

The sleeping room is down the hall from my office. Better not take off my dress. The box bed has a rubber mattress cover under the sheet that crinkles when I turn over. Stale, overheated air kick-starts a headache but the window won't open. It doesn't matter. As soon as my eyes close my head spins. There will be no sleep for me tonight. Outside it has stopped snowing. Below my window the forensic unit's parking lot and the knoll behind the hospital look white as an empty canvas in the light of a pole lamp. Peace, cold air, that's what I need. I pull on my boots – there is a stairwell next to my room – and go down, out into a new, silent, untrammelled world.

Cold pricks my cheeks, stiffens the fabric of my dress, raises goosebumps on my arms and legs. My body wants to run in circles, open its mouth to the sky and let loose. SO ANGRY!

Not possible. Patients sleeping behind the banks of curtained windows above me have been given sleeping medications but what if one of them should get up, or a duty attendant should happen to look out, or worse, slip out for a smoke? I shiver, my breath vapourizing in the floodlit air, and hear my own therapy room voice:

Let's examine this anger. What is its cause?
ERNIE!

And a stupid job that has me running from crisis to unsolvable crisis!

And a justice system that would make me responsible for the ruination of a deeply troubled woman.

And me. Why can't I do better than this?

Uncorked, anger reveals itself as a container, of what toxins?

FEAR: It puffs out into the freezing night. Of what exactly?

Conflict. Chaos. Normie's problems. What they are doing to Kay.

My lack of control. My need. My desire.

For Ernie?

No! Yes. For young, quick-to-laugh, warm and sexy Ernie.

Tough luck, Dr. Duck. I try to shake the tension out of my shoulders. My shadow in the floodlight, its legs long as stilts below a stubby giant's body and head, shakes with me. I wave to her. An arm long as spaghetti waves back. I raise both arms, flailing, my outsized fingers dancing on the snow like the legs of a giant upturned bug. I jump, hear a laugh. And now my shadow and I are shimmying towards the lamp pole, turning sideways to the light, bums thrusting up, laughing hard now, twirling in loops around the parking lot on skinny stilt shadow legs, gulping in air, until my shivering makes me stumble up onto the knoll at the edge of the parking lot where I lose my steak and wine and Sex on the Beach.

4 am: I wake up under a heap of hospital blankets in the box bed and there, glowing like a pearl, is the answer to my conundrum about Cailey. So simple, so right.

My job as a forensic psychologist is to search each accused person's psychic sea, looking for a branch of logical coral on which to anchor a life-altering decision. But if our laws are the ships society uses to navigate these stormy seas of chaos, it is the captains, not the boats, that determine our direction. I had forgotten that.

Seven

My skirt suit and blouse in muted blues, pantyhose and chunk-heeled shoes lend Cailey the look of a reasonable, sane, sallow but only slightly life-beaten person. Seeing herself in the washroom mirror, she snorts.

"You're the one looking for freedom." I hand her a hairbrush.

"Whatever you say, Dr. Boots-of-the Day."

Another couple of hours and she will be free. Charlie Forman, who acts as duty counsel, has struck a plea-bargain deal with the Crown Attorney on my recommendation. All we need, he told me, is to put the case before a judge willing to follow me through the labyrinth of facts and psychology and regulations to the only just conclusion: a discharge conditional upon Cailey's agreeing to seek long-term therapy. Sherry Freeland, a new, young judge who drives into town on Fridays, is our best bet. If she agrees – Charlie says there is no doubt about that – Cailey will not be saddled with a criminal record and once released, will stand a much better chance of defending herself against any repercussions from the Stan incident, should the need arise.

Katrina, a policewoman who handles court services, will drive her to the courthouse and give her breakfast in the holding cells. I will follow in my car and prepare to make my statement. Cailey's job is to look respectful at all times, contrite if she can manage it.

Sleet, which has been falling since before dawn, has laid a slippery sheen on everything. Cailey teeters down the slippery steps to the parking lot. No need for handcuffs, the prisoner can barely keep her balance. Needles of ice strike our faces.

The four-lane highway has one travelled rut in each direction, rain freezing on contact with the windshield, wipers scraping. I put on the radio: Golden Oldies, Janis Joplin's raunchy blues voice singing about freedom. And I see myself the other night, shimmying and shaking around the parking lot with my weird, elongated shadow. Being my shadow, waving its spaghetti arms, stepping out of my ordered, uptight self. Free to be who I honestly, truly was. Full of pain, but it felt right. Ahead of me Katrina's police car is crawling down the icy highway, taking Cailey towards her freedom. And now I see her ancestor Deirdre running through the Nova Scotia forest, having her outrageous red cloak idea and then acting on it.

"'Cos nothin' ain't worth nothin' honey, if you ain't free."

Behind me a dark blue Lexus pulls out to pass. Seriously? In this? I take my eyes off the road long enough to glance through its passenger side window. The driver on his cell phone! Passing Katrina now, his back wheels sway left. The driver overcorrects. The Lexus goes into a spin. Sideswipes the police car. Its back end skids sideways. Katrina's brake lights flash on-off, on-off. The Lexus spins again. Slams into Katrina's driver's side door, metal on metal crunching, screeching in the freezing air, the police car careening to the right, spraying slush. Its front end topples off the shoulder of the highway into the ditch, its rear wheels, airborne, still spinning. The Lexus comes to a halt facing me, the driver's face frozen in disbelief as the distance between us closes.

I have been tapping my brakes. My car fishtails but holds the road. Stops a foot from the Lexus. Behind me the road is empty, thank God. I pull off, call 911 and open my door. Bitter wind off the river whips me with sleet. My red boots are not made for walking on ice but Katrina's car is only a few feet away, its nose jammed into dirty, crusted snow and last year's dead weeds in the ditch. Pellets of ice beat a tattoo on its roof. The driver's door has been squashed inwards, the windshield a mess of cracks.

"Katrina?"

No reply. An airbag has her pinned behind the steering wheel. Locked behind a metal grate in the back, Cailey looks shaken but safe.

The Lexus driver is standing at the edge of the road. Behind him cars carefully skirt his car, which is still facing the wrong way.

"Get your car jack," I shout to him, "Maybe we can pry open this door!"

He does not move. Sirens arrive: paramedics,

a policewoman, fire fighters carrying steel jaws-of-life. Awake now and protesting, Katrina is shepherded into the back of an ambulance. Cailey sits in my car wrapped in a blanket. The policewoman is talking to Lexus Man. I go over, show her my credentials, look into Lexus Man's pampered twenty-something face, and take vicious pleasure in reporting the cell phone.

I will take Cailey to court, I tell the officer. "I'm her doctor and you have your hands full here." Her car is parked a hundred feet behind mine, lights flashing. A policeman in a second car is setting up cones, waving the early morning traffic into the passing lane. "Don't worry. She's not dangerous and will probably be discharged."

Behind its fogged up front window, the greasy spoon across from the court house is a hive of coffee smelling warmth and chatter as lawyers, court staff and those looking for justice fuel up for the week's last tangles with the law. Soaking wet, hair hanging, I choose a table at the back, near the end of the counter stools. I should have delivered Cailey to the court house cells, to impress upon her one last time that this is the future for those who wantonly break the law. Instead I tell her the homemade tea biscuits here are the best in Canada.

"So go crazy." She has been locked up, first in jail, then with me, for nearly a month. Before that she lived in a ravine. Even without this morning's accident, the free world's bustle would have come as a shock. She is looking furtively around her. "My treat," I tell her.

A platter of bacon and eggs and pancakes goes by.

"I'll have that."

"Me too." I grin, surprising myself.

While we wait I explain to Cailey what exactly will happen in court, how the legal process allows room for Justice and circumstance to find harmony, how I can find her 'criminally responsible,' but that does not mean she must be convicted because the Crown Attorney, apprised of the extraordinary nature of this case, has agreed to a 'conditional discharge.'

Cailey listens intently. The waitress delivers our breakfasts.

"What if that judge doesn't –"

"That's why the hearing is today, in front of young, fair-minded Ms. Justice Sherry –"

A briefcase drops with a bang onto the counter next to us. Jerry Delainey, the town's busiest defence lawyer, slumps onto the stool beside it.

"Damn it to hell, Elaine, did you put a spell on this freezing rain-soaked bag of a morning?" Jerry and I cross paths whenever he thinks one of his miscreants might benefit from a mental disability assessment. Sometimes I concur. Today I can find no banter.

The waitress pours him a cup of coffee. He bathes his jowly cheeks in its rising steam. Becomes aware of the silence and runs his eye over Cailey, then me.

"God's teeth Elaine, did you and your friend get run over?"

'Friend.' Both Cailey and I do a double take at the word.

"Just about."

Fortunately men like Jerry don't want to hear anyone else's story. He nods, sips his coffee.

"Damn weather. I line up the easy-riders on Fridays – biff, bam and they're back out on the street – but apparently sweet Sherry does not drive through freezing rain." He empties his coffee cup, picks up his binder. "So old Hammer Head's standing in."

"What!"

"My sentiments exactly." He tosses some coins onto the counter. "Better go find my client a suit of armour."

So in the end a sleet storm is going to determine the course of justice for Cailey Armstrong. Old Hammer Head, the supernumerary judge who started us on this odyssey, should have been put on a cruise ship to the Land of Nod years ago. Read him a pre-sentence report and his eyelids flicker, mind struggling, his memory all but gone. Favourite expressions are his refuge: 'An example must be made ...' 'The community must see ...' Discretion, consideration, compassion do not live in Hammer Head's Swiss cheese of a brain. He will not begin to comprehend, let alone countenance our conditional discharge agreement. And break and entry, a Criminal Code offence, carries one of the widest ranges of penalty, all the way from a suspended sentence with probation to life imprisonment.

"What's up doc?" Cailey has stopped chewing.

The waitress, hovering with the coffee pot, catches sight of my boots, steps back for a better look.

"Nice statement: little red boots dancin' in the freezing rain. Good for you."

Dancin' in the rain... and in the snow, pirouetting the other night in the hospital parking lot.

The waitress is still here, waiting for something? Cailey glances at me then turns to her.

"You'll have to excuse her. We nearly died on the way here."

"Jesus! Really? Well God's in a snit today, that's for sure." She puts her free hand on Cailey's shoulder. "Still, you made it, so you must be doing somethin' right." And I see us through her eyes: two thirty-something women in business suits sitting over breakfast.

Women disguised: Me as my shadow. Deirdre and the others in front of Chester's blockhouse on that pivotal morning two hundred and thirty some years ago. Daring to use what they had, and imagination, to defend against the breakdown of law and order. Trembling inside their inside-out cloaks as back and forth, back and forth they marched, risking everything.

"Are you okay, Doc?" Cailey glances up

at the clock. The restaurant is beginning to empty, people jockeying to pay their bills at the cash register in time to cross the road and get settled before court convenes.

Concern, for me. From a vibrant, intelligent woman about to lose the only things in life guaranteed to deliver salvation to any of us: freedom and love. Her journey has deposited her here, in the lap of my trust. But, doctor of the human psyche, hunter of truths, the only thing I know for sure this morning is that I have never risked anything much, never battled and cried, played and made love like Deirdre. A week has passed since Chez Henri. Ernie and I have not spoken. Over the weekend skating/gymnastics/laundry/groceries/a leaky toilet/a sleepover for Kay/a tantrum for Normie, who I swear is an emotional weathervane, left me neither the time nor the inclination to force a connection with Ernie, and his first line of defence is to not respond. Who am I then to measure the energies moving through the woman across from me? And there is no chance now of justice coming to Cailey through me. If I take her back to the unit and her case is put over, who knows what judge will decide it?

"Isn't it time?" she asks.

My 4 am idea has a cousin. It comes to me now. Has no scruples apparently.

I reach into my handbag under the table. So many laws line up against what I am about to do. If I lift my hand, pass its contents across to Cailey, I will be guilty of shirking my custodial obligation to the court. We will both be guilty of fraud. Criminally responsible? Yes.

If caught. Because who, in my humdrum little life, will connect a freezing-rain morning when Dr. Elaine Price, chief of St. Christina's forensic unit, sat in this coffee shop with what is about to happen?

Freedom means drawing lines in the sand, choosing what to do, creating our lives, and there is no return from a moment of action to the moment before it, to the safety of a life run by 'oughts' and 'nots' and 'shoulds.' But to do nothing, to watch the system grind carelessly over Cailey, will rot us both, from inside. Cailey is right, acting without personal responsibility, accountability, that is the definition of evil. 'Professional objectivity' is a coward's phrase.

Watching me, Cailey smiles uncertainly. The counter stools, the tables around us are empty now. The waitress has retreated to the kitchen.

"Listen to me." I lean across the table. Luckily, last night I withdrew six hundred dollars for groceries, tomorrow's market, and a hospital's fund raiser. I pull it out along with my car keys, slip the money and keys into my napkin and push it across the table to Cailey. "I'm going to the washroom now. You take these and go. Park my car in the lot behind Union Station in Toronto. Leave the keys under the seat. I'll take the train in later today to pick it up." The words speak themselves.

How sweet it is to see her shock. But now

her head begins to shake, her ponytail flapping wetly against the shoulders of her suit.

"No no no, you can't do this, you'll get into so much –!"

"Shh." I look around us, then explain what is certain to happen to her in Hammer Head's court. "The justice system is only as good as the people running it, Cailey. It can be pretty hit and miss. So go. They won't miss you until your name comes up, and then," I widen my eyes, frown, perplexed, apologetic. "'I'm sorry, Your Honour, I went to the washroom …' Hammer Head will become apoplectic –"

"But doesn't helping me make you guilty of a crime too?"

"Only if police can prove I broke the law." Glee/fear is spreading heat up into my neck and cheeks. "My choices are mine to make, Cailey. And since when has legality been an issue for you?"

She sits there, fear a stubborn guard. Tendrils of her hair, beginning to dry in the restaurant's muggy heat, have sprung out of her ponytail, giving her a harried, helpless look. I try to help.

"It's your only option, as I see it. And actually it came from you." I grin.

She stares, speechless. I love it.

"Deirdre, her creativity, is what brought me the idea –"

"I made her up, Doc!"

"Maybe, but the historical record is there.

What you did was bring it and her to life, I think because your own life is broken. That's also why you broke into that house. But it is my considered opinion that what you did was neither criminally responsible nor insane." The words feel solid, unshakably true down in the centre of me. "Our family stories, who our mothers and fathers and ancestors were and the forces that worked on them, are woven into who we are. You know this better than most of us." I sit back, certainty a birth existing in its own right moment, free of the need to deliver anything other than itself. "So get with the scheme, Dream Team. Go find your man. Then think about all of this, because the day will come when you need more than a tent in a ravine, you know that too. But next time you decide to change your circumstances, come to see me first. There'll be time enough then to sort out the legalities."

She examines her coffee cup. All I can see are her eyelashes. Time ticks us closer to her appointment in court. When finally she looks up, for the first time since I've known her, I see tears welling.

"Why are you doing this for me, Doc?"

"Because you are a royal pain in the ass and I can't wait to get rid of you." I smile.

The waitress drops off the bill and I get up, take my first steps into the no-man's-land outside the law. Cailey is watching, I know, as my new red boots do a little one-two step on their way across the restaurant.

Eight

A late spring snowfall is turning the world white again as I write this. Poor robins, just returned, will have spent the night huddled against the freezing trunks of the fir trees, the strongest in the innermost sheltered spots, weaklings teetering on the outside branches. My poor spring-starved psyche would like to slit my wrists if not for Kay and Normie spilling down the stairs, shouting their delight.

"Can we go outside, Mom, just for a minute?" Kay pleading, so young this morning, the little girl I so badly do not want to lose to a cellphone and Snapchat and make-up.

"Please Mom!" Behind her Normie is bouncing up and down in his one-piece jammies with the space ships on them.

It's time to get dressed, to eat, pack lunches, negotiate snarled snow-morning traffic –

"Sure, why not, if you hurry up and get dressed." I hear myself laugh. "Can I come with you?" We might make it to school before nine o'clock. Or not.

The kids stare, not used to my being at home, wearing jeans.

"We could make a snowman in the front yard."

I have been suspended pending investigation of my actions on that freezing rain Friday. I will face a tribunal. Will I stick to my 'I needed to pee' line, placing the blame for what happened on absent Cailey? Telling the whole truth will bring me censure for unprofessional conduct, the loss of my license possibly, if there is a criminal conviction, maybe even jail time. But sitting here in yesterday's sweatshirt, I have been exploring the energy that made me pass over my money and keys that day. It was the right thing to do, and that's who I want to be, wherever it takes me.

Frosty is the same height as Normie, with grape eyes, a carrot nose, gangly dead Virginia creeper arms. I get down on my knees to take both my little son's mitted hands, my face close enough to hold his eyes with mine.

"He's beautiful, isn't he?" I smile. "But if the temperature goes up he'll melt, you're old enough to know that, aren't you?"

"Of course I am!" Letting go of me, he hugs our snowman. "Bye Frosty."

"Who says Frosty's a 'he,' Mom?" says Kay, a smile quirking.

A week later the ice leaves the river. It always happens suddenly, the water's current pushing, pushing against the weakening ice, snapping it somewhere upriver and then surging into a tumult of floes. Walking beside it, I watch its surface ripple, ever-changing patterns reflecting the sky, and think of Cailey in her tent, and wonder where I'm headed. Please god, don't let my children suffer, that's all I ask. In the meantime, while I wait maybe I'll take a leaf out of Cailey's book and go online to search for my ancestors and the lives that brought me to this moment in time. Maybe I can find my own Deirdre, to give me strength and keep fear at bay.

Soon, if I am still free, I will turn over the garden. The kids might help. Normie has not had a tantrum for nearly two weeks now, and has made a new friend at school. Kay laughs more often. And last night, after they were in bed, I plucked up enough courage to face the stone of sadness that seems always to be sitting at the bottom of my stomach.

I don't want to live with the man Ernie has become, but does that mean I have to lose him? I love the Ernie I married, and miss him. Would he listen if I told him that? Invited him out for a cup of coffee, just the two of us? Are we capable of talking openly and honestly to each other?

I wouldn't put money on our chances – what I have done will push him further away unless he loves me enough to try to understand – but our faux fur rug is still here on the floor and I haven't yet traded his easy chair for a hibiscus.

ACKNOWLEDGEMENTS

Many thanks to Dr. Dorothy Cotton, clinical psychologist specializing in mental health and law enforcement, and recent recipient of the Order of Ontario. Thanks to my family, especially to Dr. Sarah Collins, and to Grant Collins without whom this book would not have been written. Finally, thanks to Sonia D'Agostino and Luciano Iacobelli of Quattro Books for turning my story into this beautiful book.

OTHER RECENT QUATTRO FICTION

Jane Bow grew up in Canada, the U.S., Spain, England and the former Czechoslovakia. Her first writing job, as court reporter for Thunder Bay's *Chronicle Journal*, allowed her to watch justice unfold in far flung northern Ontario communities. She lives in Peterborough, Ontario.